D0962488

The News from Spain

The News from Spain

Seven Variations on a Love Story

• • • • • • •

Joan Wickersham

ALFRED A. KNOPF   NEW YORK   2012

THIS IS A BORZOI BOOK
PUBLISHED BY ALFRED A. KNOPF

Some stories from this work were originally published in slightly different form
in the following: *Agni, Glimmer Train,* and *New England Review.*

Library of Congress Cataloging-in-Publication Data
Wickersham, Joan.
The news from Spain : seven variations on a love story / Joan Wickersham.—1st ed.
p. cm.
"This is a Borzoi book."
ISBN 978-0-307-95888-4
I. Title.
PS3573.I252N49 2012
813'.54—dc23
2012005073

Jacket photograph by Stacy Renee Morrison
Jacket design by Gabriele Wilson

Manufactured in the United States of America
First Edition

"Everything that happens, happens this way, or that way, or this other way. And in each of these diverging stories all the others are reflected, all brush by us like folds of the same cloth."

—ROBERTO CALASSO,
The Marriage of Cadmus and Harmony

The News from Spain

The News from Spain

The motel was called The Sands of Time, but it could just as easily have been The Dunes, or The Sea Shell, or The Breakwater, or The Harbor Rest—all of which were the names of other, similar, motels lining the road that led to Plum Point. The rooms smelled of disinfectant and of bodies. Nothing vulgarly specific, not the smell of sweat or feet: just a tired essence of long, hard, human use. The rooms were clean, but the surfaces felt slightly sticky. Outside, the wind was dazzling and salty.

It was a Saturday. July. The Hardings, whose middle daughter, Barbara, was newly engaged at the age of forty-six, were having a party at their house on the Point, and they had reserved a block of rooms for their overflow guests.

Susanne and John got to the motel just before four. It was the first time they had been away alone together since she had found out, in April, that he'd slept with someone else. It had happened two years before—happened only once, according

3

to John, at the end of an intense friendship he'd fallen into with the woman who owned the Chicago gallery that was putting on a show of his paintings. There had been e-mails; he had flown out to meet with her several times to work out the details of the show; he had not realized, he told Susanne in April, that this kind of danger could sneak up on you. There'd been liking, maybe a little flirtation although he hadn't acknowledged this even to himself at the time; certainly there'd been respect on both sides—

"Stop," Susanne had said.

He did stop, looking sad and troubled and solicitous. He was all those things, Susanne knew. He had done it; doing it had horrified him and he'd never seen the woman again, except at the opening, when Susanne had flown out to Chicago with him. She remembered the gallery owner in a red hand-painted kimono jacket, an attractive mix of animation and steadiness. Susanne, knowing then only that John liked her, had liked her too. She wore the same perfume as Susanne's best friend at boarding school. "What is it again?" Susanne had asked.

"Chanel Number Nineteen."

"That's right."

"It's getting harder to find it," the gallery owner had said, and that had been their whole conversation, because someone had interrupted them.

Susanne had found out about it one·night this spring. A wifely moment: she'd bought him a wool shirt last Christmas, it had itched and he'd returned it, and now the store was having a sale and she was looking for the credit slip so she could get him something else. She looked through some things lying on top of John's dresser and then thought to check his wallet, where he often kept odd receipts. She'd pulled out a folded piece of paper, softened and grayed: something he'd been carrying around for a while. A printout of an e-mail. She'd read it. She'd gone into the bathroom, where he'd been getting out of the shower. After a while they had turned the shower on again, hoping to muffle things—by then he was sobbing, and she was almost screaming—but their daughter, Ella, had knocked on the door and asked what was wrong. "Nothing!" they'd both answered.

They'd been married for twenty-six years. They had loved each other since high school.

Over the past three months since that night, Ella's presence in the house had been both protection and hindrance. They'd had to keep themselves in check.

This morning they had dropped her off at a friend's house, where she would spend the night. Then they had driven north, and then out toward the coast, in silence. Susanne drove. John read a book, and then napped. A familiar drive: they used to do it all the time, when Susanne's father still had his house on Plum Point. They came to the clam shack where they always used to stop. Susanne drove past it and pulled in at a different place, a few miles down the highway. It turned out the clams weren't as good. She noticed, and she knew that John noticed. She saw him decide not to say anything and she was annoyed that he hadn't, because it deprived her of her chance to shrug coldly. She also saw the sadness of all this, the desperately angry smallness of it: the unspoken little spat averted because they both knew he'd lost the right to protest being made to eat at the wrong clam shack.

On the back wall of the motel room there was a sliding glass door. Susanne stood for a few minutes looking out at the harbor. It was almost the view she'd grown up with, but not. You could see the lighthouse from here, the whole fat white cylinder of it, and the ferry dock, the line of cars waiting to get on. From her family's house on Plum Point, three-quarters of a mile up the road, you saw the ferry only in progress, laboring into and out of the harbor, and you didn't see the lighthouse at all, only the pale wedge of its light sweeping the sky. But from Plum Point you saw the Race, invisible from here, the strange patch of water where the tides and currents crossed and went crazy twice a day. As a child the idea of the Race had thrilled and terrified her: the idea that a benign place could turn treacherous at predictable intervals. And with the dining room telescope you could see Sinnewisset, where the ferry went, and beyond it the string of small nameless purple islands.

When Barbara had called with the news that she and Barnaby were engaged, and that there would be a summer party at Plum Point, Susanne had thought that coming here would be piercingly sad: she had managed never to come back in the six years since her father had sold the house after his third divorce. But then she had found the piece of paper in John's wallet; and now she looked out at the harbor impassively, the familiar place from the unfamiliar angle, and went to hang up the dress she planned to wear to the party.

John was lying on his back on one of the beds; there were two.

Susanne surprised herself by saying aloud, "Well, so that'll be an interesting decision."

He looked at her and saw that she was looking at the beds. She'd spoken in a particular drawl that in the past had often marked the end of a fight between them: ironic, still a little pissed, but with a clearly sexy edge.

He answered, in the same drawn-out, challenging, let's-play tone: "Yes, it will."

But hearing him speak that way—his quick assumption of

something shared—made her turn away. She unpacked her things into one of the rickety stale drawers, and when she finished she said, "I'm going out for a walk."

"You can't just keep holding on to this," he said. He'd been sitting on the bed watching her. It occurred to her then that the speed with which he'd assumed a truce, which she had read as arrogance, might have had more to do with relief.

She opened the sliding door and stepped outside.

Barnaby was lying on his back on one of the beds in his room, his hands behind his head. He had folded the bedspread down; it looked so dingy and used; he hated the idea of lying on something that so many other people had lain on before him. He looked up at the ceiling, which was rough and swirly. They must have added sand to the paint. Had they done this as an extension of the beach theme, or was it just a standard motel painting practice because it showed the dirt less? It was such a relief to lie there and wonder about this kind of stuff. This kind of nothing.

He thought of his favorite line from one of his favorite movies—*Holiday*, with Katharine Hepburn and Cary Grant. When the Cary Grant character walked out on Katharine Hepburn's awful sister, and she crowed in a voice of angry ice: "I'm so relieved I could *sing* with it." That's how he felt right now, lying on his back in The Sands of Time motel with the air conditioner hissing and his shoes off and the curtains closed and the phone off the hook and the sandy ceiling and the pictures of big seashells bolted to the walls. He didn't have to talk to anyone or be anywhere for another hour and a half, and he was so relieved he could have sung with it.

"But those rooms are for overflow guests," Barbara had said.

"Doesn't that crack you up, the idea of an overflow guest?" Barnaby had asked. "It's actually a very odd concept."

"Mom's been assuming you'd stay at the house. She's got a room set aside."

"It's bad luck to have the groom staying in the house."

"That's just the night before the wedding."

"I must have read the wrong etiquette book." For some reason Barbara's literalness tended to make him goofy. Maybe he would calm down, living with her. Maybe she would learn to be goofy. The idea of a goofy Barbara was so preposterous that he had actually laughed.

"What's so funny?" she'd asked.

"Nothing. I'm just tired."

"Besides," she said, "you've stayed in the house before."

Her face was a mix of coyness and distressed appeal.

He looked away. He'd stayed with her once in her room, lying next to her in her bed. "Are you attracted to me?" she had asked that night.

"Of course I am, you're very attractive. I'm just tired," he had said. He had said this on each of the occasional nights when they ended up in bed together. He didn't know what he would say after they were married.

He picked up the remote control for the TV, which had been resting on his stomach. Saturday afternoon—there was never anything good on Saturday afternoon. Golf. Golf. Weather. Laurel and Hardy—or was that Abbott and Costello? He could never tell the difference, and all four of them gave him a headache. Golf. Bowling. *Fishing,* for God's sake. He stopped here, for a bored moment, to see what there was to see. Nothing. The guy caught a fish, held it and stretched it out in the shallow water, to show how big it was, Barnaby guessed, though he didn't see the point of this, as the fish was actually quite small; and then the fish was let off the hook and it swam away. He pressed the "info" button to see how long the show was—it ran from four to six. *Two hours.* He started to laugh, a choked barking laugh. He wanted to say to someone, "Two hours of *fishing*—can you believe it?" By the time the show was over, he would be standing on the Hardings' vast lawn in his linen jacket and his gray slacks, smiling next to Barbara, shaking hands and kissing people's cheeks and saying, "Thank you, thank you, yes, *very* happy, thank you."

He tried to think of people whom he'd be glad to see, and thought of Susanne. Barbara had said she and John would be staying at The Sands of Time too. He picked up the phone and dialed "o" and asked to be connected to her room, trying to prepare some conversational opener that would include the phrase "overflow guest." But John answered the phone. Barnaby always felt formal with John—he liked him fine but never knew quite what to say to him. John told him that Susanne had gone out for a walk. Barnaby said, "Well, please give her the message that I called, and I'll see you guys at the party."

"We're looking forward to it!" John said, with what struck Barnaby as a slightly weird heartiness, but a lot of things were striking him as weird lately.

He switched the channel and found a horse race—an hour-long show, he learned by pressing "info" again, which meant forty-five minutes of blabbing and horses walking around, and then three minutes of race, and then some wrap-up.

He hit the "mute" button and left the show on, reading the names of the horses as they came up occasionally on the bottom of the screen. *Red Dynamite. Bold Captain. Out of This World.* Boring names. He remembered suddenly that at the age of nine or ten he'd been addicted to the racing column in *The*

New Yorker—not because he'd cared about racing but because he'd loved the names of the horses. It had been the year of Majestic Prince, and his favorite had been the horse that kept coming in second. It had had the best name—which he couldn't now remember. He frowned and closed his eyes; it had been so important to him that year, so indelible, he could see the slim typeface, remember the columnist's byline (Audax Minor, another great name—he had asked his mother once, "Why didn't you name me Audax?" and she, with her habitual kindness, had explained to him the concept of a pen name)—but why couldn't he think of the name of the horse? His parents would have been able to tell him. By that point he'd been the only child left at home, and he and his parents had had long dining room lunches on Saturdays and Sundays. He remembered that room so clearly: the pale gray walls, the sunlight coming in bright and excited through the old diamond-paned windows. Barnaby had brought notebooks to the table in which he'd written lists of racehorse names he'd made up since the previous weekend. "I like that one," his father would say gravely, and then he'd listen to the next. "But maybe not that one."

"No, it sounds a little cheap," his mother would add. "Not like a Thoroughbred. More like the name of a door-to-door encyclopedia company."

"Yes, well, you had a different childhood from the rest of us," his sister Diana, who was closest to him in age but still eight years older than he, had said after their mother had died last year and he'd started crying one afternoon when they were all there clearing out the house. "I think by that point they were atoning. You were like their—it's like when corrupt noblemen used to give money to the church in their old age, because they suddenly realized they were going to die."

"You're right, Diana, that's exactly what it was like," Barnaby had managed to tell her coldly. The conversation had enraged him then, and it enraged and desolated him to think of it now. It had been the beginning, for him, of a particular kind of loneliness: the kind that comes from remembering something wonderful, knowing that you're remembering accurately but forgetting some of it, and knowing that there's no one left who can corroborate or complete the story.

Susanne and John had to wait at the little guardhouse while the guard looked up their names on the Hardings' guest list. The guardhouse had always been there, in the middle of the narrow strip of road that marked the beginning of Plum Point, and the guards who manned it—old men, retired policemen—had always known her, always glanced up and waved as she'd walked or driven past. She didn't recognize this one, and there was no reason why he should have known her, but it bugged her. She felt like saying something loudly to John for the guard to overhear, something that would demonstrate an insider's knowledge of the place ("Did you notice the Swains have put a new wing on their house?"), but she kept silent. The guard found their names and nodded.

"What's this like for you?" John asked, as they walked up the road, toward the Hardings'.

"It's fine," she said. (And thought: *If you know me so well, if you care so much, then how could you, why did you,* which seemed to be the destination—rhetorical, exhausting—of a lot of her thinking lately.)

Ahead of them was the party, the sloping green lawns stretching out from the Hardings' big white house in all directions, clusters of dressed-up people. Susanne and John walked slowly up the driveway, which peeled away from the main road just before the curve that led to Susanne's old house and which also kept it invisible from here. She was rounding that curve in her mind, the whole time she was walking away from it up the Hardings' driveway, remembering the tall holly hedges that stopped suddenly, so that suddenly you saw the house, the rambling angles of it mirroring the curves of the road, its front side low and dull because all the excitement was at the back: the long stone veranda, the lawn, the flowerbeds, the flagpole, the wild roses, all that green, all that color, the flag snapping in the wind, the rope slapping against the flagpole, the pale bright blinding light of the harbor.

Oh, house.

They came up to Mr. and Mrs. Harding, standing on the grass below the front porch ("What's her name again?" John murmured, just before they got there. "Mrs.," Susanne said. "When we're sixty and they're ninety, it'll still be Mr. and Mrs."), who peered at them and kissed them and said to Susanne, "So wonderful to see you back here," and asked after her father. Then came Barbara, in a cream-colored strapless dress. She kissed Susanne; and Susanne, rattled by the dress, which seemed both too bridal and too young, said, "This is just so great!" "We have you to thank," Barbara said, laughing, and Susanne said, "Really?" And Barbara said, "Remember? We met at your dinner party. You tried to fix us up." "But it didn't work," Susanne said. "Sure it did—it just took twenty years," Barbara said, laughing.

Then came Barnaby. Susanne hugged him and smelled cigarettes and toothpaste. "How are you?" she said into his ear.

"Heavily medicated," he said into hers.

·   ·   ·

After a while people stopped arriving, and Barnaby asked Barbara to excuse him for a moment. "Sure! Sure!" she said brightly; this party seemed to be exciting her and making her even stiffer than usual. There were two bathrooms on the ground floor, but Barnaby went upstairs, down the hall past Barbara's room to the big bathroom that looked out over the bay, which had shimmered earlier but was growing dark blue and rough now as the evening came on. He locked the door—an old-fashioned hook that dropped into a metal loop screwed into the door frame, just the way the bathroom doors had locked in his parents' house in Brigantine—and opened the window, sat down on the floor, and lit a Marlboro Light. Even if they figured out later that someone had been smoking in here—a smell in the towels, in the curtains—they wouldn't know who it had been. He hoped no one out on the lawn happened to look up to see puffs of smoke emanating from the window: A new pope has been chosen, he thought.

When he'd finished his cigarette, he flushed the butt down the toilet and put some toothpaste on his index finger and rubbed it around inside his mouth. He looked at himself in the mirror and saw that his expression wasn't that different from Barbara's: hectic and wooden. He smiled, then tried to smile again more naturally and ran his tongue over his teeth to get rid of what was left of the toothpaste, which was pale green.

On his way back down the hall he heard women's voices coming from the bedroom of one of Barbara's sisters. ". . . and I said, 'Why don't you wait awhile, you don't have to get married right away, maybe you should live together first,' but she didn't want to hear it."

"Do you think he's gay?"

He kept moving, and ducked into the next bedroom, which was Barbara's. He'd had a feeling they all wondered about that—maybe even Barbara did. But it was awful to hear them actually talking about it. He was breathing heavily, shaking with—what? Rage? Shame? He never looked at men, and the idea of actually sleeping with one disgusted him. But so did the idea of sleeping with a woman. Not just Barbara, any woman. This had not been true when he was younger: he'd had some perfectly nice sex with nice women who, after a while, would want to marry him, which ended the relationships—not because he'd pushed these women away or fled them but because they got sad and discouraged after a while and left. He'd probably had a low sex drive to begin with, and now that he was older he seemed to have lost the ability to desire, the way people could lose the ability to diet or sing or write poetry. But how long had he felt this way? Since his parents had died, or since before then? His last, lukewarm, love affair had been seven years ago, and his parents had both died in the space of the last three. A diagnosis of grief seemed, Barnaby thought—and was aware of the irony of remembering, just then, his mother's passion for anagrams—at once too pat and not apt.

John got them drinks. They milled around. Susanne talked to people she knew from Plum Point, and people she knew from college, where she and Barnaby had met and become friends. She got into a conversation with a woman who turned out to be the owner of her family's old house, and who thought Susanne would want to know about all the changes she'd made. At one point during this, she glanced around and saw John talking to a white-haired man in a seersucker jacket—the party was full of white-haired men in seersucker jackets—and he looked back at her. They'd always had this sort of radar in a crowd; they each knew where the other was, and could telegraph something that wasn't a greeting but more like a checking-in: *Still there?* *Still here.*

It had all its old sweet power, she found; it was undiminished—but it was accompanied, too, by something else: a sadness, maybe a wariness. A kind of gingerly self-congratulation: *You see? We can still do this.*

Hands came down on her shoulders from behind. She turned to see Barnaby. "You look beautiful," he said. She thanked him. He said, rapid and overanimated, "No, really. I've been standing over there thinking about who would paint you, and I decided Bronzino."

She smiled, and he said, "No, see, that wrecks it," and she wanted to say to him, *Oh, Barnaby, calm down, what is it?* But the very tightness with which he was wound, the thing that was making her worry about him, made it impossible to get anywhere near him. It was the party, she thought, and she said to him, "Do your cheeks hurt from smiling?"

He said, "God, I wish I could sit with you at dinner."

"But you can't."

"I'm at the dignitaries' table."

"That's because you're a dignitary."

"A foreign dignitary."

"Really?"

"Visiting from another planet."

"Oh. Well, then: welcome."

People were beginning to move down the lawn toward the big striped tent, that glowed in the deep-blue evening with candles and lantern light. Susanne saw Barbara walking toward them, holding her skirt up off the ground with one hand, picking her way carefully across the grass in high-heeled sandals.

"Listen," Barnaby said to Susanne, his eyes on Barbara, "let's have an assignation later."

"What?" Susanne said, not mistaking his joking tone for anything else, but still startled.

"We're both staying in that same shithole place. I'm in room two-twelve. Come knock on my door around midnight, okay?"

Then Barbara was with them, smiling, tucking her hands around one of Barnaby's arms. "Hey, you two," she said.

They started to walk down toward the tent.

"It's a beautiful party," Susanne said after a minute; the silence had begun to feel like it needed to be broken.

"I'm so glad!" Barbara said.

"Are you cold?" Barnaby asked, looking down at her. "Would you like me to get you a sweater, or a wrap or something, before we sit down?"

"Thank you," Barbara said. "There's a wrap on the chair in my bedroom. Light green," she added, as he headed off.

She turned then, and put both her hands around Susanne's arm as she had around Barnaby's. They walked very slowly down the lawn, in a way that was part saunter, part march. They didn't say anything. Susanne kept expecting someone to come and break in on them with cheery party talk, one of the guests sweeping past them on the way to the tent, but no one did. They just kept moving, separate and quiet. She crossed her other arm over her chest and put her hand on top of one of Barbara's, which was still clutching her. Susanne rubbed the back of Barbara's hand in small circles.

"Remember Vikram?" Barbara said suddenly.

"Vikram?" Susanne remembered an angry-looking, sullen, handsome man around whom, for several years, Barbara had built dinner parties. He'd been a political scientist from Oxford, here on one of those fellowships that seemed to go on for a surprisingly long time before ending with what seemed like surprising suddenness. Susanne had found him pompous and difficult to talk to. She also thought he'd been a creep to Barbara, neither returning nor clearly refusing her love, sitting at her table, eating her meals—such elaborate food, prepared so nervously and determinedly to delight him—and being rude to Barbara and only slightly less rude to her friends. Barnaby, Susanne remembered, had always been the extra man at the dinner party, the one invited in case he might happen to hit it off with whatever single woman friend Barbara had invited that evening. He had talked lightly and easily, frowned slightly when Vikram stung Barbara, drawn out the single women without in the least leading them on, praised the food, helped Barbara clear the table. "What about Barnaby?" Susanne had said to Barbara at one point, after Vikram had gone back to England and married someone to whom, it turned out, he'd been engaged for years. "Barnaby? No." Barbara had actually shuddered. "I feel like he's hanging around on the ground with his mouth open, waiting for me to finally drop off the tree."

"Of course I remember Vikram," Susanne said now.

Barbara held Susanne's arm tighter, nestling into her side. "Nobody liked him, did they."

"It just seemed like he wasn't very nice to you."

"He wasn't, really. But—oh, you know." They kept slowly walking on the lawn. Barbara laughed a little. "I guess he was just the one that got away."

"Well," Susanne said, automatically soothing, still rubbing Barbara's hand, "maybe we all have someone like that."

They had almost reached the tent. Barbara drew away and stared at Susanne. "What are you talking about? You married the one who *should* have been the one that got away."

.   .   .

If they had happened to look up at the bathroom window, they would have seen that another new pope had been chosen.

Bad behavior. He knew this. He was forty-seven. He was an executive vice president in charge of corporate communications for a mid-size financial services company.

He rubbed his mouth with toothpaste again, went down to dinner, put the wrap gently around Barbara's shoulders, and then sat down and took hold of her hand under the tablecloth. The look she gave him—benevolent, relieved—made him want to cry.

At dinner Susanne talked to the man sitting on her left— a conversation that never lifted off from the factual where-were-you-born stuff, made harder by the fact that both of them were trying so earnestly to get it off the ground. "And your wife?" Susanne asked. "Is she from Michigan also?"

Waiters came and took away the soup plates and put down plates of rare beef and two tiny roasted potatoes.

The woman on Susanne's right turned out to be a college friend of Barbara's. The conversation began pleasantly, but then suddenly the woman, who'd had quite a lot of wine, said, "So why is she marrying him, do you think?" She smiled at Susanne—she had straight black hair and delicate, deep eye sockets, a weary, cold sort of beauty. "I'll tell you my theory," she went on. "She has these two sisters with their marriages and children and their establishments—not just households, *establishments.* And she's watched it all for years, and now she's tired."

Susanne nodded and looked across the table at John. He was talking to the man next to him, but he saw her look and got up and came around the table and crouched by her chair. She touched his shoulder lightly and stood up, and he followed her out of the tent. The orchestra was playing "I've Got You Under My Skin." Soon people would start dancing.

"This is an awful party," she said.

"Do you want to leave?"

"We can't. Not yet."

Along one side of the Hardings' lawn, where it sloped down to the bay, there was a tall yew hedge. Susanne headed for the spot where she thought the opening would be, groped, found it, and walked through. As kids they had called this "the Maze." It wasn't really, because there was only one possible route through it, but it had felt the way they imagined a maze would: a narrow angled passage whose green walls were too high to see over and too dense to see through. As she and John walked through it she told him about what the drunk woman had said at dinner, and about her conversation with Barbara. For some reason she didn't mention what she and Barnaby had talked about.

"You don't *do* that!" she said, going back to the drunk woman. "You just don't. You don't *say* things like that to a stranger at a party." (She was a little drunk herself.)

"No," John said, "but you're also upset because you think she's right." (His own slight intoxication often showed up this way, a concise, clear-eyed gravity.)

They ended up kissing each other, for a long time, standing between the high yew walls. *Oh God,* he kept saying, *oh God.*

Susanne felt split: kissing him, watching herself kissing him. *God*, he said against her collarbone.

She didn't want to walk any farther; the Maze eventually opened onto another flat patch of lawn, from which you could see her family's house, and she didn't want to see it. They went back to the party for a while and had champagne and dessert—a kind of round chocolate thing with ice cream inside, which looked like a small cannonball and seemed intended to be emphatically not wedding cake and thus to remind people that this party, despite all its eager nuptial trappings, was part of the build-up, not yet the real thing. The drunk woman had disappeared, so John sat next to Susanne and she gave him most of her cannonball. They watched Barbara and Barnaby dancing, correct graceful dancing-school steps executed while smiling into each other's faces in the way that had also been encouraged, though rarely adhered to, in dancing school. Then, when other people got up to dance, Susanne and John walked back to the motel and got into one of the beds.

For the first time in all those months, she took him in her mouth. She heard him crying; and then realized he wasn't crying. Then he tried to reciprocate, and she said, sharply, "No!" and they both froze, she because she was wondering, again, what exactly had gone on in that bed in Chicago, and he because he knew what had gone on—and now, suddenly, feeling him tense, so did she. There was a long, still, dangerous moment, but she pulled his mouth to hers, and got her hips against his, and things went on with a roughness that was only partly fueled by rage and sorrow.

Barnaby and Barbara, too, ended up kissing in the Maze. She led him there, after the party had petered out (which it had by eleven—he'd known it would be an early night). She held his hand, she turned her face up to his, and he kissed her, even paying dutiful attention to the places where her skin stopped and the bodice of her strapless dress began. Her flesh quivered; she sighed; he felt sorry for her and angry at himself.

"I love you," she said.

"I love you too."

Was it immoral for them to say these things, to marry each other? So much was missing—not just from his side, he knew, but from hers, too, from the way she felt about him.

But they both wanted to get married. They were both tired of not being married. After twenty years of intersecting social life, in some ways they barely knew each other. He'd thought for a long time, somewhat seriously but mainly idly, that from a distance she looked right. This thought had become more urgent in the last year or so, and lately she'd begun to think the same thing about him. They were standing out in the moonlight now and his mouth was prowling around her cleavage, but they were still at almost the same distance.

In bleaker moments he had thought: She could probably, at this point, marry anybody. The problem was that he was somebody—she was marrying a blank, but the blankness was something that, in the close and daily proximity of marriage, he would be unable to keep up.

"You do?" she asked.

John had fallen asleep, sprawled on his back on top of the sheets. He was snoring. Susanne got out of bed and looked at him. She looked at her watch: it was ten minutes past twelve. She pulled on some clothes, the jeans and T-shirt she'd worn earlier that afternoon. She found the room key where John had dropped it on the dresser and let herself out, closing the door quietly behind her. She had started to climb the wooden staircase that led to the second floor of the motel when she saw that Barnaby was coming down toward her.

"Hey, Susanne," he said. He seemed startled to see her.

She said, "Did you forget our assignation?"

"Our assignation?" he said blankly. Then he said, "Wait a minute, that didn't sound very gallant, did it."

"Barnaby," she said, "it's a joke."

He came down the rest of the stairs and took hold of her forearm. "Let's have our assignation on the beach."

They passed out of the margin of light around the motel. The moon was up and the beach was pale and bleached; it was easy to see where they were walking. Barnaby still had on his clothes from the party, but Susanne shivered and he gave her his jacket. It was loose, and warm from him. He put his arm around her, and they walked a little way down the beach. Then they sat down on the cold sand, and Barnaby said, "Excuse me," and held his jacket away from Suzanne's chest and pulled a pack of cigarettes out of the inside breast pocket.

"Want one?" he asked. She shook her head, and he lit one for himself while she cupped her hands loosely around his to protect the match from the wind. (They both, simultaneously, had a sudden memory of how, at Barbara's dinner parties, when Susanne had still smoked and Barnaby had smoked openly, the two of them used to go out on the doorstep together and stand beneath the small porch hood, struggling to light up in the rain, in blizzards, that small, innocent, exciting touch of their hands.) It took him a few matches, but finally he drew in his breath and blew out smoke.

He said, "All right, if you won't smoke, then what about—"

and then Susanne felt his hand fumbling near her hip and he pulled something out of that pocket, something heavy that she'd noticed dragging on the jacket when she'd put it on. A silver flask. She laughed.

"What?"

"Just that you're so well equipped."

"I know. Did I think I'd find myself unexpectedly fox hunting?" He unscrewed the lid. "Actually, with Barbara's family, there could be fox hunting, couldn't there."

Susanne drank some brandy, loving the deep stabbing burn of it, and passed the flask back to Barnaby.

"So," she said.

"So."

They sat looking out at the luminous sky, and at the harbor silvered by moonlight.

That was when they would have talked, if they had talked. Barnaby might have told her that he knew his engagement looked shaky from the outside, but that he was counting on Barbara's discretion and rectitude to make the marriage work. He might have said that he believed that after a point Barbara would stop wanting and stop asking, that she'd decide the marriage was what it was and would consider it a point of honor to uphold it. That he didn't know anyone else with whom he thought he could build a marriage on honor, and that it was the only thing he thought he might possibly build a marriage on. That he was afraid of being alone if he didn't marry her, and if he did. That he missed his parents; that no one knew how much; that he knew that even he didn't quite comprehend how much.

And Susanne might have told him about John. (She hadn't told anyone, except for her mother, and that had been an accident, something that had burst out of her mouth one day when her mother was going on, as she so often did, about how wonderful John was and how Susanne should appreciate how lucky she was to be in that marriage.) She might have told him that she was tired of being angry at John, that it was fading a little but that she didn't think it would ever stop. That she wondered if it would always go on this way or would eventually change: this paradox that any moment of happiness between them became a new, incendiary part of the grievance. That the times, like this evening, when it was good again made his having fucked someone else seem even more pointless.

They sat on the beach not talking. In a way they didn't trust each other. It had nothing to do with thinking the other person wouldn't understand—he knew that she would have, and she knew the same of him. It was thinking that the other person's understanding wouldn't really make any difference. Maybe they were right, maybe it wouldn't have. There was something comfortable, and symmetrical, about sitting there together thinking they knew how deep their trust in each other—or in anyone—could go, and where the limits were going to be.

After a while Barnaby picked up a big shell, a whelk. "When I was growing up we had a house on the Jersey shore." He smiled; Susanne saw his tired face relax in the moonlight. "And my father would hand me a shell and say, 'Want to listen to the news from Spain?' Because we were roughly across the Atlantic from Gibraltar. I used to love that, thinking that if we went out in a boat the next place we'd hit would be Spain."

Susanne took the shell from him and held it to her ear. An urgent tumbling whispering roar. A sound unheard for years, but old, instantly familiar. A sound from childhood: you thought that if you could only listen hard enough you'd be able to decipher what you heard.

Barnaby had found another shell for himself, she saw.

And then for a long time—longer than they would have expected, though neither of them said this aloud—they sat and listened to the news from Spain.

The News from Spain

The news from Spain is terrible. A bomb under a park bench in a small town near Madrid. Fifteen people have been killed and dozens injured. Harriet tells the aide, who crosses herself; the nurse, who says, "It makes you want to stay home and never leave the house—but that would just be giving in to terrorism"; and her daughter Rebecca, who says, "Why do you spend all day watching that stuff?"

Rebecca is tired. Harriet has been sick on and off for years, more than a decade. Rebecca has just driven four hours from Boston to get to the Connecticut nursing home where Harriet now lives. She is taking two days off from the small bookstore she owns, paying her part-time assistant extra to cover for her. She's brought a shopping bag full of things Harriet likes: rice pudding with raisins, shortbread, fresh figs, and a box of *lamejuns* from a Middle Eastern bakery. She has walked into the room and Harriet has barely looked away from the TV to say hello.

What Harriet says is, "They just interviewed a man whose granddaughter died in his arms."

Rebecca puts down the shopping bag and kisses the top of her mother's head. Someone has given Harriet a haircut, a surprisingly flattering one. Her head smells faintly of shampoo.

Harriet puts up a hand and feels for Rebecca's face, briefly cupping her chin. "They think it was a Basque separatist group."

Rebecca nods and goes down the hall to the kitchen, to put the rice pudding and *lamejuns* in the fridge. The hallway is full of wheelchairs, a straggly becalmed flotilla of gray people just sitting there, some with their heads lolling on their chests. On the way back to her mother's room, she runs into the social worker assigned to Harriet's case. Today is Halloween; the social worker is wearing a pirate hat and an eye patch. "How do you think your mom is doing?" she asks Rebecca.

"I think she's still angry about being here," Rebecca says. Harriet moved into the nursing home a month ago, after the rehab hospital said she had "plateaued," and the assisted-living place said they couldn't take her back.

"I know," the social worker says. "But they adjust."

When she goes back into her mother's room, Harriet is watching for her. The TV is off. "I'm so glad you came," Harriet says.

"I just ran into the social worker in the hall. She says you're adjusting."

"Bullshit," Harriet says. "Did you bring stuffed grape leaves?"

"I didn't remember that you liked them."

"I love them."

"Next time," Rebecca says. She pulls over a chair and sits facing her mother. Harriet is in a wheelchair, paralyzed again—it has happened before, she has some rare chronic spinal disease, but this time the neurologist says it is permanent. Rebecca, who came down to go with her mother to that appointment last month, listened while he talked to Harriet about suffering and acceptance, about how what was happening to her was truly terrible, worse than what anyone should have to go through. Rebecca liked the doctor's humanity, and thought it might be somewhat comforting to Harriet; certainly Harriet has always found it gratifying to be admired for her bravery. But Harriet was furious. "He's talking philosophy when what I really want to hear about is stem-cell research."

Rebecca feels guilty about not making it down to see her mother more often. Harriet is always mentioning something she needs—lavender talcum powder, or socks, or an afghan to put over her legs when they wheel her outside, or, she sighs, "just a really good turkey club sandwich." Rebecca mails what she can, alternately touched by and annoyed by the many requests (are they wistful, or reproachful? Both, she thinks). (But they are also, simply, practical. These are the small things we live with, and Harriet now has no way to get hold of them.) She has talked to Harriet about moving to a nursing home in the Boston area. "It would be more convenient."

"For you, you mean," Harriet said. She is adamant about staying in this particular nursing home, because the man she's in love with is in the assisted-living place next door, and comes over to visit her nearly every day. Rebecca thinks it's great that her mother has someone, though she could do without some of Harriet's more candid reports ("Ralph called me this morning and said, 'I wish I could make love to you right now'").

"How is Ralph?" Rebecca asks now.

Harriet shrugs. "He thinks I'm mad at him because he didn't give me a birthday present."

· ·

"Are you?"

"Yes." They laugh. They talk. Rebecca heats up some *lame-juns* in the kitchen microwave and makes Harriet a cup of tea. They hear the woman in the room next door say loudly, angrily, "Who washed my floor?" A low murmuring answer; then the angry woman again: "In the future I must ask that you not wash my floor without first giving me notice."

Rebecca looks at Harriet. Harriet says, "At first I thought, Oh good, at least she sounds like she has all her marbles. But that's all she ever says, on and on, day and night about the floor."

Some *lamejun* has fallen onto the front of Harriet's sweatshirt; when she finally notices and brushes it off, it leaves a spot. "Damn it." She wipes furiously away at it, but in the midst of the fury is also grinning ruefully at Rebecca—*Can you believe it? How does it happen every single time?* She's a very large woman, and she's been dropping food on her shirt for as long as Rebecca can remember. The last time Rebecca visited, on the day Harriet moved to the nursing home, the aide swathed Harriet's front in an enormous terry-cloth bib before bringing in her dinner tray. Harriet allowed it, looking at Rebecca with a kind of stunned sadness; of all the enraging indignities of that day, this was the one that undid her. "She doesn't need that," Rebecca told the aide.

"We do it for everybody."

"Right, but my mother doesn't need it."

So that was one small battle that Rebecca was there to win for Harriet. Without Rebecca, Harriet could have won it just fine for herself. Both of them knew this—and yet, between them, love has always had to be proved. It is there; and it gets proved, over and over. Some of their worst fights, confusingly, seem to both prove and disprove it: two people who didn't love each other couldn't fight like that—certainly not repeatedly.

Still, Rebecca has often wished for something quieter with Harriet. Are there mothers and daughters who can be happy together without saying much?

"You know," Harriet says now, frowning, clearly resuming an argument she's been conducting in her head, "you jump on me about watching the news all the time, but it's not because I'm just some morbid tragedy hound, it's—"

"I know why it is," Rebecca says.

Rebecca's younger sister, Cath, disapproves of the relationship between Rebecca and Harriet. She thinks it's unhealthily close. She says she is tired of giving Harriet inches and having her take miles. (Rebecca, who has never seen Cath give Harriet an inch, finds this declaration both funny and infuriating.) Cath is a sculptor and lives in Denver. She thinks Harriet is a monster. She thinks—and here Rebecca agrees with her—that their father, a quiet, scholarly, self-deprecating man who drank, had ended up drinking more and walling himself up more and dying lonely because Harriet took up so much room. Harriet always had another man, single, recently divorced or widowed. "She had affairs," Cath said. "She broke Daddy's heart."

"You think those were affairs?" Rebecca asked, remembering all those wistful, mostly handsome, young men who had always seemed to her to be intruding—what were they doing at the Thanksgiving table? Why were they hanging around on Christmas Eve?—eagerly passing the cranberry sauce and trying brightly and unsuccessfully to engage her father in conversation.

"Not *consummated* affairs," Cath said, with exasperated authority. "Mom was never brave enough, or radical enough, to actually sleep with anyone else. Those affairs were all about noble renunciation of actual sex. They were all about deprivation and suffering."

She has said, more recently, to Rebecca over the phone: "She's going to live to be a hundred, you know. People like that, who only care about themselves, live forever, because every ounce of energy they have goes into preserving the organism."

Rebecca and her mother had begun to get close only when, nearly fifteen years ago, Harriet seemed to be dying.

She was diagnosed with stage four colon cancer just when the revelations broke about the rotten marriage of the Prince and Princess of Wales. Rebecca was going through her own fierce divorce at the time (it had started amicably, with a mediator, and then escalated to the point where the lawyers' bills had become so horrifying, so disproportionate to whatever it was that she and Steve had been fighting over, that the two of them had met for a drink one night and agreed to do everything the mediator had suggested in the first place).

But when Harriet got sick, Rebecca picked up the phone and called her soon-to-be-ex-father-in-law, who was on the board of a famous cancer hospital. She believed that Steve's father, who had never liked her much and had never done much to conceal his dislike, was nonetheless fundamentally ethical and would do what he could to help. (Another belief, both bitter and accurate, was that he liked to remind himself of his own power by pulling strings and making things happen.) He got Harriet admitted to the hospital, and the surgeon who was supposed to be brilliant lived up to his billing.

The doctor came and spoke to Rebecca after Harriet's surgery, which took an entire day. "I got it all," he said, and went on to list all the places where he'd found it: pretty much everywhere, as far as Rebecca could tell.

"So what's her prognosis?" Rebecca made herself ask, though she felt she already knew.

The surgeon looked seriously at her. "I have no idea," he said.

Rebecca wanted to hug him for that, and would have hugged Steve's father, if he had been there. She did hug Steve, who had showed up unexpectedly at the hospital and sat in the waiting room with her all day. They had spent most of the time hunched over a book of Sunday *New York Times* crossword puzzles; they screwed up each one irreparably, in ink, and then they would make a big blue *X* on it before moving on to the next one.

During that day, and right afterward, Rebecca thought that maybe the divorce was a mistake, and that she and Steve would get back together. But it turned out to be like the illness of Anna Karenina: a kind of temporary exalted goodwill, a glimpse of how lovely things might have been if everybody hadn't felt the way they actually did feel.

She went out and bought *People* magazine, and a copy of *Diana: Her True Story*. Every day she read to Harriet, who lay in bed with tubes coming out of her nose and puffy boots inflating and deflating around her legs at automatic intervals, to prevent blood clots. "She tried to kill herself with a *lemon slicer?*" Harriet said. "What's a lemon slicer? Do they mean a peeler? She tried to peel herself to death?" The two of them sat there in the dark hospital room, laughing. Whenever the surgeon came in, Rebecca hid the book and the magazine in the nightstand, because Harriet didn't want him to think she was the kind of woman who read trash.

Harriet would later say of that time, "It was a nightmare."

Rebecca, who, partly in reaction to her mother's hyperbolic way of putting things, tends toward understatement, would say, "It was tough." But while it was going on, it was, in some bizarre way, also wonderful. They liked being together, for the first time in years. One afternoon, a couple of days after the surgery, Harriet needed a blood transfusion. The drip was still running when someone, mistakenly, brought in a dinner tray. Harriet was not allowed to have anything by mouth, and so Rebecca told the aide: "We don't need that."

"Oh, you've eaten already?" the aide said.

Harriet, lying on her back with the blood still dripping into her arm, raised her hands and curved them into little bat claws and said, in what Rebecca somehow understood was meant to be a Transylvanian accent: "I'm still eating."

Rebecca laughed, and her eyes filled with tears at the valiance of it, the surprise of that sudden little flash of wit.

It was before Rebecca started the bookstore; she was teaching high school English then, so she had the summer off. She went to the hospital every day and stayed there all day.

Then Harriet went through her year of chemotherapy. Rebecca was teaching again, but she went down to Connecticut on a lot of weekends. The pope got colon cancer. They watched the networks grappling with the delicate challenge of reporting on a pontiff's gastrointestinal system: lots of disembodied scientific diagrams juxtaposed with footage of worried-looking nuns praying in Saint Peter's Square.

"What do you think the nurses are saying to him right now?" Harriet said, lying on the couch and looking at a shot of the outside of the hospital where the pope had been operated on earlier that week.

"Okay, Your Holiness, scoot your heinie over to the edge of the bed," Rebecca said.

Harriet laughed and laughed. Then she threw up.

So here's the glib psychological explanation: Harriet had always craved attention and now, made vulnerable by illness, needed more; Rebecca had failed at her marriage and needed to feel like a hero.

All of which was true. But it was more that they both discovered, almost shyly, that they liked each other. That they were having, in the middle of all this dire stuff, a good time together.

It was also, Rebecca knew, that her mother was dying. She sometimes lay in bed at night and cried, alone, or with Peter Bigelow, who taught architectural history at Harvard and whose two children—he was divorced—went to the school where Rebecca taught. He held her and listened while she talked about how hard it was to be finding her mother and losing her at the same time.

But, Peter said, it sounds like the knowledge that you're losing her has been part of what allowed you to find her.

Oh, he was a nice man, Peter. Back then, her romance with him felt too new. Too soon embarked on, after Steve (though she and Steve had been separated for nearly two years by the time Peter asked her out to dinner). Too green and slight to bear the weight of everything Rebecca was feeling back then, about her divorce, about Harriet. Poor guy, she had thought, looking at Peter's kind, earnest face, his sandy rumpled hair, his open, trusting bare chest, his kind hand resting on the sleeve of her flannel nightgown.

Are you sure you don't mind, if we don't, tonight?

Of course not.

I'm sorry, I thought I wanted to, but—

Rebecca. Don't worry. It's fine.

His tenderness seemed almost unbelievable to her. She might have been suspicious of it, seen it as his need for heroism, or as a ploy to hook her before revealing his true, selfish self (remember, she was just wrapping up a divorce). But she'd seen him for years with his kids. He was nice, period. He cared for her without being maudlin or nurselike. He took her out to dinner and to concerts, talked to her about his work enthusiastically and not at all pompously (he was writing a book on H. H. Richardson), listened while she talked about wanting to quit teaching to open a bookstore, and was frank and relaxed in bed.

He advised her to pace herself with Harriet. Her friends were saying the same thing, especially the ones who'd had sick parents. Go easy, take time for yourself, don't let this take over your whole life. Rebecca thought she was pacing herself, some. She was still driving down to Connecticut almost every weekend, but she was also teaching, and seeing Peter, and getting together with friends. But her mother was dying, and Rebecca wanted to cram in as much as she could. In some unexpected way she and Harriet had fallen in love.

Incredibly, Harriet didn't die. Her cancer never came back. She kept having more surgeries: to insert a catheter for the chemo drugs under her chest wall, to remove it again because of recurrent infections, to remove scar tissue in her abdomen, to remove more scar tissue. Rebecca kept driving down and spending time with her mother.

The glow wore off.

What a disconcerting thing to feel, to acknowledge! It wasn't that she was sorry Harriet was still alive. It was more that she couldn't keep it up: the attention, the rapport, the camaraderie, the aimless joy of just hanging around with her mother, watching the news. She had burned herself out, just as Peter and her friends had warned that she might; but looking back at the time when Harriet had seemed to be dying, she couldn't imagine having managed it any other way.

Harriet started feeling that Rebecca wasn't visiting often enough. It was true, she was coming down less often. But, oh, that "enough." That tricky guilt-laden word that doesn't even need to be spoken between a mother and daughter because both of them can see it lying there between them, injured and whimpering, a big throbbing violent-colored bruise of a word.

"What about Easter?" Harriet asked—plaintively? Coldly? In a resolutely plucky way that emphasized how admirably she was refraining from trying to make Rebecca feel guilty? It could have been any of those ways of asking, or any of a number of others, all of which did make Rebecca feel guilty, and angry, and confused about whether to say yes or no. Part of the burnout took the form of an almost frantic protectiveness of her own time whenever Harriet wasn't sick. If her mother needed her, she dropped everything and went; if her mother didn't need her, she wanted to feel free to say no.

Harriet, on the other hand, seemed to feel that the time Rebecca spent caring for her didn't count. Hurting, drugged, frightened, throwing up—that's not what Harriet called spending time with her daughter. (The watching-the-news part was engrossing, and sometimes fun, but it was more like a jailhouse party, a desperate entertainment concocted by people who have very little to work with.) Harriet wanted to travel with Rebecca—to go on a cruise to Alaska or the Panama Canal. Or to see Moscow and Saint Petersburg, for heaven's sake—all those mythical places that you could now, suddenly, actually go to.

Rebecca had no desire to travel with Harriet, and she was getting ready to start her bookstore, looking for space, making a business plan, applying for loans. *"A bookstore?"* Harriet said. "With your education you want to start a store, and one that doesn't even have a hope of making money?"

"It's what I care about," Rebecca said.

"I worry about you," Harriet said. "What is your life adding up to?"

Rebecca was hurt, furious. What did a life, anyone's life, add up to? Why did Harriet feel she had a right to say things like that? (In her head, Rebecca wrote the script for what a mother should say in this situation: "That's wonderful.") They had one of their old fights, made worse by the fact that Rebecca hadn't realized these old fights were still possible. The recent, long entente around Harriet's illness had lulled Rebecca into a false sense of safety. She felt ambushed.

Then Harriet sent Rebecca a check, for quite a lot of money. *To help with the bookstore,* she wrote on the card.

"You can't afford this," Rebecca said.

"It's what I want to do," Harriet said.

Then she got sick again.

Pneumonia—not life-threatening, but it took a long time to get over. Rebecca drove down, and made Harriet chicken soup and vanilla custard, and lay across the foot of Harriet's bed watching the vigil outside the Fifth Avenue apartment building where Jacqueline Onassis was dying. They watched while John Kennedy came out and told the reporters that his mother was dead.

"Poor Jackie," Rebecca said.

She was remembering how much her mother had admired and pitied Jackie in the years after JFK's assassination, when Rebecca was growing up.

But, "What's poor about her?" Harriet said. "She's been living with another woman's husband."

37

· · ·

So this has been going on for years. Harriet ailing and rallying. Rebecca showing up and withdrawing. Living her life between interruptions—which, she herself knows, is not really a fair or accurate way to characterize it. Harriet has been sick a lot, needed her a lot; but most of the time she has not been sick or needy. Most of the time, Rebecca is relatively free. Maybe, then, it's that Rebecca doesn't feel that she's done much with her freedom. That each interruption points up how little has happened since the last one.

She runs her bookstore, quite successfully. She tried opening a second store in a nearby suburb, but it did not do well; the experiment was stressful but not disastrous; after a year she closed the new store, paid back the loans, and felt relieved.

She's been seeing Peter for a long time. They enjoy each other. They trust each other. They spend a few nights together most weeks, but both of them like having their own apartments. His kids went away to college; his ex-wife remarried, and so did Steve. Early on—a couple of years into their relationship—Peter asked Rebecca how she would feel about getting married. That was how he did it: not a proposal but an introduction of a topic for discussion. She said she wasn't sure. The truth was that when he said it, she got a cold, sick feeling in her stomach, and that was the thing she wasn't sure about and didn't want to look too closely at. This lovely, good, thoughtful man: What was the matter with her? She was nervous, and also miffed that he seemed so equable about the whole thing, that he wasn't made desperate by her ambivalence, that he wasn't knocking her over with forceful demands that she belong to him. On the other hand, she wasn't knocking him over either.

Then his book on Richardson was finished, and published.

He brought over a copy one night, and she had a bottle of champagne waiting, "Peter, I'm so happy for you," and she kissed him, and they smiled at each other and drank, and she kept touching the cover of the book, a very beautiful photograph of the Stoughton House on Brattle Street. "*Peter,*" she said, and he smiled at her. Then he went into her kitchen to carve the chicken, and she began to flip through the book. She turned to the acknowledgments page, and her own name jumped out at her: ". . . and to Rebecca Hunt, who has given me so many pleasant hours."

It was understatement, wasn't it? The kind of understatement that can exist between two people who understand each other? (The kind she was always wishing for, and never getting, from Harriet.)

What did she want: a dedication that said, "For Rebecca, whom I adore and would die for"?

Here was something she suddenly saw and deplored in herself, something she seemed to have in common with Harriet: a raw belief that love had to be declared and proved, baldly, loudly, explicitly.

She saw the danger, the wrongness, of this; yet when Peter came in from the kitchen, carrying the chicken over to the table Rebecca had set in front of the fireplace, she said, "Pleasant? Is that what I've given you—many pleasant hours?"

"Some unpleasant ones too," he said, humorously, nervously—he saw, suddenly, what was coming, and he was trying to head it off.

What came, though, that night, turned out to be not so bad. Rebecca was able to rein it in; she didn't need to harangue him, or freeze him, although they talked less at dinner than usual. Peter said, "You know, I'm not sure what made me choose that word, but it was probably not the right one."

"That's okay," Rebecca said, and it was, really. What they had together *was* pleasant.

But still the word continued to bother her, whenever she thought of it. The fact that it appeared to be lauding, but the thing that it praised was a limitation. Thanks for not getting too close to me. Thanks for not getting too deeply under my skin. Peter had disowned it somewhat, said it might not have been the right word—but Rebecca thought that it was probably not so much an aberration as it was a revelation: one of those sudden, sometimes accidental, instances when everything is brightly lit and you see where you are. Long ago, in her marriage, there had been moments like that. Rebecca had had a friend back then named Mary, whom she'd since lost touch with; they'd been close for a couple of years when they'd both been trying to keep sinking marriages afloat. One night they had sat on the front steps of Rebecca's apartment building, talking about their husbands, and Mary had said, "You know those things in the beginning—the things that bother you and you tell yourself, 'Oh, that doesn't matter'? I'm realizing now: all of it matters."

Rebecca and Peter, of course, aren't at the beginning. They're more than ten years in. And isn't that the problem, really—that they are so far in, and yet not far in at all?

"Where do things stand these days with Peter?" Harriet is always asking. She means: Why don't you marry him? Or, if you don't love him enough to marry him, why don't you move on and find someone else? (Both questions are unspoken; but the second, nevertheless, carries all the buried force of an ultimatum: if you're too stupid to appreciate Peter, give him up, and *then* you'll be sorry.)

She asks again on the Halloween when Rebecca visits her

at the nursing home: the day of the bombing in Spain, the *lamejuns,* when Harriet is supposedly "adjusting." It's about a month after Peter's book has been published; he has sent down an inscribed copy for Harriet, which she holds in her lap, stroking the picture of the Stoughton House.

"Things don't stand anywhere," Rebecca tells her. "Things stand where they always stand."

She goes down again a month later, for Thanksgiving. She would like to take Harriet out for dinner, but this is impossible, because Harriet can't go anywhere except in an ambulance or a wheelchair van, either of which would cost several hundred dollars. So they sit in Harriet's room and eat nursing-home turkey, with very wet stuffing. Then there is pumpkin pie—not too bad—and dark chocolate pastilles, which Rebecca has brought because Harriet loves them.

"I had a very strange conversation with Cath," Harriet says. "She called me, and she asked me why, when you girls were little and I would take you to a Broadway musical, why wouldn't I ever buy you the original cast album when they were selling it in the lobby."

"What did you tell her?"

"I said I didn't remember. Which is the truth." Harriet looks at Rebecca, puzzled. "Do you think she's in therapy?"

This makes Rebecca laugh, and after a moment Harriet snorts, too, and the two of them end up wiping away tears, trying to collect themselves.

The legs of Harriet's stretch pants have ridden up, and Rebecca notices a bandage on her calf.

"It's infected," Harriet tells her when she asks. "It got

bumped on the wheelchair, and I asked them to put some anti-biotic ointment on it, but they never got around to it."

They play Scrabble; Harriet is still pretty good. From some-where down the hall, a woman begins to moan. The same words over and over: *Take me home. Please, please take me home.*

"She does that all the time," Harriet says, her hand hovering over the box of tiles. "I don't know if she thinks her children are in the room with her, or if she's talking to God."

"Either way," Rebecca says, somber, not even sure what she means by "either way."

But Harriet makes it explicit. "Either way, she's not crazy to want it; and either way, it isn't happening."

A man has been coming into Rebecca's bookstore every couple of weeks. He buys a lot—no specific category, he just seems generally ravenous: novels, poetry, history. He is short, prob-ably in his late fifties, with silver-rimmed glasses and a large shaggy graying head and a big square jaw that reminds Rebecca of a lion. He grins at Rebecca when he pays. They don't talk. Their not talking, which might at first have been shyness or reserve, has begun to feel deliberate, erotic. His name, on the credit slips, is Benjamin Ehrman.

Already Rebecca can tell the story two different ways. One ends with them getting married. The other ends with her look-ing back over a cratered battlefield of a love affair and wonder-ing: What were you *thinking*?

Harriet calls late one morning, practically in tears.

"What is it?" Rebecca asks.

"I'm still in bed. They haven't—when I woke up I said I

needed the bedpan. And the aide told me it was too much trouble, I should just . . . go, and they'd come clean me up. So I did, but that was a couple of hours ago—"

Rebecca looks at the clock hanging on the wall of the bookstore. It's eleven-thirty. "I'll call you right back." She hangs up, and then calls the nursing home and asks to speak to Harriet's caseworker. She describes what Harriet has just told her, and ends by saying, "That is not okay."

"No, it's not," the caseworker agrees smoothly. "You're right. But sometimes they can make it sound worse than it really is; there may be a little more to the story. Let me go look into it."

Rebecca's hands are shaking. "I don't think my mother is confused about what's going on." She keeps picturing the caseworker in her Halloween costume: her eye patch, her blackened tooth, her little plastic dagger. And she says again, "This is not okay."

She hangs up and calls Harriet back. "The social worker is sending someone to help you."

"I'm sorry."

"Mom. *I'm* sorry." They stay on the phone until Harriet has to hang up because, she says, "Here everybody is, all of a sudden."

Benjamin Ehrman comes in and buys the *Oresteia* and the complete Ecco Press set of Chekhov stories. Is he taking some sort of middle-aged Great Books course? Is he courting her, trying (successfully) to slay her with his taste?

He pays. He smiles. He doesn't say anything, not even thank you. At the point when any other customer would have said "thank you," he smiles at her again.

Oh, Rebecca, you tired, confused woman. You are so ripe for this kind of thing.

She goes down to visit Harriet at Christmas. (She and Peter have never spent the holiday together; she always goes to Harriet, and he is either with his kids or off skiing in Utah. This year, the separation bothers her. Not in itself—she hates skiing—but the fact that there is no expectation that they will make a plan together. How could there not be, after all this time? On the other hand, doesn't the ease with which they go their separate ways—the pleasantness of it—confirm that she is free?)

She brings Harriet a beef tenderloin she has cooked, and she reheats au gratin potatoes and green beans in the kitchen microwave. The gray people in their straggly hallway flotilla watch, or don't watch, as she walks by holding dishes aloft. One woman looks at her and raises a forefinger, like someone timidly hailing a cab. "Excuse me," the woman says, "but is this Washington Square?"

"No, it isn't," Rebecca says.

"Do you know how to get there from here?"

Rebecca shakes her head, and the woman smiles and shrugs.

Harriet says of the dinner, "You can't imagine what a treat this is."

"Yes I can," Rebecca says. "That's why I brought it."

Ralph's children have taken him out for dinner—they all live nearby—but later that evening he comes to see Harriet. Rebecca likes him: he is blunt and loyal, and quick, like Harriet.

Rebecca sits, trying to straighten out a piece of knitting (a red scarf, Harriet's Christmas present to her, which, Harriet says, "should have been done ages ago but I keep screwing it up—you know I'm not domestic"), while Ralph and Harriet play anagrams on a table rolled up against Harriet's wheelchair. They take turns flipping over a new letter and seeing if they can steal a word the other person has already made.

Rebecca, ripping out rows of Harriet's impatient thwarted knitting, is nearly in tears, watching them: the speed, the sureness with which they play. Ralph steals "risked" from Harriet, adds his own "T," and makes "skirted." Harriet steals "donuts" and makes "astound."

One Sunday afternoon, in the middle of January, Rebecca goes to the movies by herself. She stands in line—a long one—not thinking of much. The smell of popcorn, and how sickening it is. The fact that the hole in the right-hand pocket of her orange wool coat has now become big enough that she ought to start carrying her loose change in the left one. Ahead of her in line a man is waving, beckoning, smiling. Benjamin Ehrman. She turns around to see if he means someone behind her; he grins, and points at her, and beckons again. So she goes to him.

"What movie are you seeing?" he asks, and she tells him, and he says, "Me too."

She says, "So, you do know how to talk after all"; she feels like a jerk as soon as it's out of her mouth.

But, "I know," he says. "One of us was going to have to break that silence." That sounds meaningful, erotic, again; he defuses it by adding, "It was getting to be like those staring contests you have when you're a kid."

So they go in together, sit together, are deferential about the armrest, are aware of exactly where each other's hands are in the darkness. The movie is a "little" one that has received doting reviews. The audience is enraptured with it, laughing, sighing. Rebecca hates it. She looks over at him and he looks back and rolls his eyes at her. They don't know each other well enough to agree to walk out—they don't know each other at all, so walking out would mean going their separate ways. They stay, sitting there through the whole thing, grimacing at each other, sinking down in their seats, their shoulders growing conspiratorially closer as their silent agreement that the thing just stinks grows more and more intense. At the end they throw themselves out into the street, laughing. They go for coffee but order wine instead.

A list of what shocks Rebecca, over the next weeks and months:

Bed. That something she's done a lot of and enjoyed in the past could feel so fiercely new.

Underwear. He likes it, so he buys it for her and she starts buying it for herself. Tarty, expensive stuff. And nothing in her objects—not the feminist part, not the shy part, not the part that is aware of weighing fifteen pounds more than she did in college.

Her hair. It's long, it nearly reaches her waist; she's always worn it up, or in a braid. He wants it down. She sits on the bed between his thighs with her back to him, and he brushes her hair, crooning to her. And she loves it—she, who has always disliked having anyone touch her hair since childhood, when Harriet used to yank a brush through it and say impatiently, when Rebecca flinched, "You have such a tender *scalp*."

Pet names for each other. We won't even put them in here, because the ones they make up are so incredibly silly.

Italian chocolate eggs with toys inside. He hands her one

after dinner on one of the first nights he cooks for her. She thinks, Oh, how nice, a chocolate egg. When she unwraps it and breaks off a piece, she discovers a small plastic capsule inside; when she opens that, she finds six plastic pieces; when she puts the pieces together, they make a tiny pterodactyl holding a jackhammer. Oh, he says, the pterodactyl road crew ones are the best.

Jealousy. He is separated but not divorced. Rebecca sees the wife around Cambridge, a narrow pretty greyhound of a woman, with a face that is at once anxious and arrogant. She looks rich. She is rich, because Ben is rich. Five years ago he sold his dot-com company and made the kind of money that can scatter people all over an expensive city in big houses: one for himself, one for his parents, one for a son and daughter-in-law, and then another one for himself when he moved out of the first one and left his wife alone there. That had happened a year before Rebecca met him. Rebecca hates seeing this woman—Dorinda. After a sighting she always has a sense of belated, alert panic, the kind you feel when you narrowly miss having a traffic accident. She sees Dorinda in the supermarket, and Dorinda's eyes hold hers for an instant and then sweep coldly away. Is this just one person registering the presence of another, unknown, one? Or is it the snubbing of a rival? She asks Ben if Dorinda knows about her. Ben says he's mentioned to Dorinda that he's seeing someone but that they've never discussed whom. Implying that they do still discuss some things. What things? What do they talk about? How often? How married are they? There is also another, much earlier, wife: Carol, the mother of Ben's three grown children. She lives on Martha's Vineyard. Rebecca doesn't know what she looks like and is not bothered by her as she is by Dorinda, though it does worry her some that there are two of them, two of Ben's former loves cast adrift in the world. Does it mean she will one day be a third? Is he a serial discarder? No, she tells herself: he is fifty-seven, he's had a life. Rebecca is forty-five, and has a past of her own. Her quantity is equal to Ben's: two. Steve, who had grown less and less interested in sex, and eventually told her that it would be okay with him if she wanted to go out and have an affair; and then Peter.

She has of course by now broken up with Peter, who, she thinks, barely seemed to notice. In fact, it's Rebecca who has failed to notice. She is so far gone, so deeply drunk on love, that she doesn't notice how surprised and hurt he is; how aware he has been, over the years, of his own caution and reticence; how miserably, suddenly, certain he is that their long civilized mildness was fatal and largely his fault; how far from mild he is feeling now. He's angry at her but angrier at himself.

"We could still see each other sometimes," she said vaguely, cravenly, at the end. (She was thinking that it had been so friendly all along, maybe it could just keep being friendly.) "I'll miss you."

"No. Don't call me. Don't call me again unless you mean it," Peter said; and then he amended it to: "Don't call me."

It was very clear and clean, Rebecca thought at the time. They had met for a cup of coffee in Harvard Square, and they were done and she was walking home within fifteen minutes. She was relieved that there hadn't been a scene, but also not surprised. She did feel sad: she *would* miss him. She passed the store that sold the chocolate eggs, and went in and bought one to hide somewhere—Ben's slipper, the piano bench. They've taken to stashing them all over his house for each other to find.

What does Harriet make of all this? Nothing. Rebecca hasn't

told her. She doesn't know what Harriet would say, but she knows she doesn't want to hear it. She doesn't want to hear anything from anybody.

She wants to be utterly alone with Ben: she wants to drink him, eat him, climb inside him, run away with him. She's never felt this way about anyone.

What she has always thought, watching friends of hers disappear into similar love affairs in the past, is "Uh-oh."

But who is ever able to apply to her own current love affair a word like "similar"?

She gets calls from the nursing home. "I'm just calling to report that your mother fell this morning. She slid down out of her wheelchair. She wasn't hurt."

"We're calling to let you know that your mother is in the emergency room. She has a pretty high fever, and the doctor was worried she might be dehydrated."

She calls Harriet. "Mom?"

Harriet says she's okay, or she's tired, or she's mad that they didn't take action sooner, or she knows they're short-staffed and that it's not their fault, or that they're a bunch of stupid uncaring assholes who just want her money. Rebecca murmurs and soothes, gets indignant, calls the nursing home to complain, suggests to Harriet yet again that they hire a private aide to keep a closer eye on her (which Harriet has always refused to do, because as it is the nursing home is gobbling up her money and once it's gone she'll have to go on Medicaid and have a roommate, the idea of which she finds abhorrent).

Rebecca is so competent by now whenever there's a crisis. She always has been—but it's different now, more automatic, because she has Ben. When something happens with Harriet, she does what needs to be done, but it feels more like Honor Thy Mother than it does like running into a burning building to save someone you love who is trapped inside.

"And you're sure you don't want me to look for a place near Boston?" Rebecca asks.

No, Harriet always says, because of Ralph.

She talks to Cath occasionally, and Cath says, from the safe distance of Denver: "It's time for her to live closer to one of us."

(Rebecca is tempted sometimes to say: *Okay, Cath, I've arranged to have Mom med-flighted out to you.*)

Harriet gets a urinary tract infection, another leg infection, bronchitis.

She has been sick now for so long, this has all been going on forever. Rebecca wishes it would all just stop—but the only thing that will stop it is Harriet's death, and she doesn't want that.

She asks Harriet one afternoon—it's when Harriet is in the hospital with bronchitis, and Rebecca has driven down to Connecticut to spend the afternoon with her (just the afternoon: she wants to be back in Cambridge again by bedtime)—"Aren't you tired of all this?"

"Yes," Harriet says. "But I don't want it to be over, because I want to know the end of the story."

"What story?" Rebecca asks.

"All the stories," Harriet says.

"You're so sad," Ben says, rubbing the backs of his fingers against her cheek when she gets home from the bookstore one evening.

• •

"My mother's in the hospital again. Septic shock. Another urinary tract infection, which I guess they didn't catch fast enough. I'm going to drive down there tomorrow."

"I'll make you a drink," he says, and then he calls her one of the incredibly silly pet names, which for the first time fails to delight her. It seems irritating and ill timed. "And then I'll run you a bath," he says.

"A bath sounds good."

"And I'll come watch you take it."

"Come talk to me, you mean?"

"No. Watch you."

That's an aberration, not a revelation, she thinks. Being objectified, when she just wants to be accompanied.

"You're so sad," he keeps saying. It starts as sympathy. A week or two later it's cool, a diagnosis. Then it becomes a criticism.

He starts wanting the underwear to be kinkier. And he wants her to wear it every time.

He used to talk a lot about divorcing Dorinda. But it's been months now since he's mentioned it.

Rebecca asks him about it one night, as they are lying in bed, happy, she thinks, naked, with scraps of underwear scattered all around them.

"I would love to marry you," she says, with a boldness that is new and luxurious for her. She's echoing something he has said to her many times by now. "I hate it that you're still married to someone else."

He is silent. Then he says: "You knew I was married when we started this."

She tries to get out of it without too much self-abasement. She knows the uselessness of asking questions. She manages to sound less desperate than she is—but still, it's more desperate than she would like to sound.

Women ask for explanations, over and over, when love goes. There is no explanation. The explanation is: It's gone.

The whole thing, from the time they met at the little movie to the end, took sixteen months.

Back in her apartment, she's cold. It's a cold spring, wet, dark. She doesn't cook, she doesn't sleep well, she doesn't read, she doesn't see many friends. She gets her hair cut to just below her jawline, knowing it's an angry, masochistic thing to do, but hoping that it will somehow make her feel better. (And also because she can't bear now to attend to it: shampooing, brushing.) She talks to two people, her assistant from the bookstore, who has had something of a front-row seat for all this—she used to raise her eyebrows at Rebecca all those months ago when Ben would come in, buy books, and leave without saying anything—and an old, kind friend from the school where she used to teach. Both of them are kind, in fact, but both of them seem to be saying without saying, "What did you expect?" (In fact, they're not saying this. They've been watching Rebecca all this time with some concern, because she has seemed so engulfed in Ben and remote from everything else, but they have also been rooting for her, wanting it to work. The "What did you expect?" is coming straight from Rebecca herself, spoken in a voice not unlike Harriet's.)

Summer comes, then fall. Rebecca still can't walk by the store that sells the chocolate eggs.

"What's wrong?" Harriet asks over the phone. Her voice is feebler these days, hoarse.

"Nothing," Rebecca says. "I'm just tired."

"You want to hear something shitty?" Harriet asks.

"What?"

"They've stopped giving me physical therapy. They say I'm not making any progress. I said, 'Well how the hell am I supposed to make progress if you stop giving me physical therapy?' But you want to hear something wonderful?"

"What?"

"When Ralph comes over, he moves my legs for me. And he makes me do arm exercises. So I don't atrophy."

The nursing home calls.

"We're calling to let you know your mother is in the hospital again—she had a fever, and so we sent her over to the ER."

The hospital calls. Harriet has another urinary tract infection that has gone undiagnosed—she can't feel any pain, because of the paralysis—and once again she's in severe septic shock. They're putting her on antibiotics.

Harriet calls. Her voice is weak and shivery but animated, excited. "Oh, my God—did you hear about the tunnel?"

"What tunnel?"

"It collapsed. Turn on the TV. It just happened, at the height of the morning commute, they said."

"Where was this? What city?"

"I don't know. It was my roommate's TV, so I couldn't hear very well, and then the nurse or someone came in and shut it off. But it sounded awful. People were killed, they think some people may still be trapped in their cars. You need to turn it on."

"Mom, we don't even know where it's happening."

"It's in a commuter tunnel. The main one that leads to the city, they said. Or maybe it was the bridge that collapsed, the bridge that leads to the tunnel. But *everybody* goes through the tunnel."

That night the hospital calls. Harriet's fever isn't coming down. They're going to try a different antibiotic.

Early the next morning, Rebecca is trying to decide what to do—call in the assistant, or close the store for the day, so she can go to Connecticut? Stay here and keep in touch with the hospital and Harriet by phone?—when the hospital calls again and someone tells her in a clear, soft voice that Harriet is dead.

She sits there.

.   .   .

She needs to call Cath. (Who will say, "Do you think we need to do a funeral?")

She needs to call Ralph. (Who will cry. Who will be heart-broken. Who will now begin to decline very fast.)

She wants to call Harriet.

It has all gone on for so long without Harriet dying that Rebecca lost track of the fact that Harriet was going to die.

Guilt: if she hadn't gotten tired and distracted—if she hadn't let herself be so easily dazzled—if she had not relaxed her vigilance, this would not have happened.

Even in the moment, she recognizes this guilt as irrational, bogus; but it pierces anyway.

Harriet died when Rebecca wasn't looking.

She sits there.

She wants to call Harriet, more passionately than she would have believed, an hour ago, that it was possible to want that, or to want anything.

The only other person she finds she wants to call—and of course she can't—is Peter.

She will, though. Not now. Not until almost a year from now.

She will wrestle during that time with questions having to do with forgiveness. Can she forgive herself for what she did to him?

(For the most part, yes. The two of them made their polite,

inhibited, explosive mess together, she believes; it ended the way it might have been expected to end, although the particular trigger could not have been predicted.)

(But oh, the folly of that particular trigger.)

Can he forgive her? No way to know. She puts off the phone call for so long partly because she is afraid to find out.

She keeps pitting his final "Don't call me" against his penultimate "Don't call me again unless you mean it," trying to figure out which one carries more weight.

And she gets tangled in that "unless you mean it." Which she didn't even really hear in the coffee shop when he said it; which she has discovered in her memory since then. Unless she means what? She can't define it explicitly, the thing that Peter insisted she had better mean—but she does feel she understands what *he* meant by that insistence, and it gives her hope.

By the time she finally does call him, she will know that she means it, even though it will be a scary phone call to make, and even if she still won't be capable of saying clearly what exactly it is she does mean.

Harriet would have been quick to tell her, accurately or inaccurately. To guess, to analyze, to explain, to make predictions. Harriet was always the one who wanted to talk about the news, from Spain, or from the Vatican, or from some uncertain city where something had collapsed—from any place, really, where anything of interest might be going on.

The News from Spain

THE OTHER GIRL

She was small, sullen, dressed in a short skirt and white vinyl boots, wearing pale lip gloss.

She was the only other girl in the boys' school.

She didn't smile when you were introduced. "I'll show you where the ladies' room is," she said; and before you knew it you were standing inside it with her. It was the kind meant to be occupied by only one person. "I'll wait outside," you said, and she said, "Why?" and lifted her skirt and sat down.

She was your age, thirteen. She was rich, you saw when you went home with her one day after school. A young blond man, who worked for her mother, picked you both up after study hall and drove you to her house. A big new house, like a ranch on a TV show—new wood, a huge staircase with too many spindly banisters, lots of red plush. There were horses, and there was an indoor swimming pool, and a pantry full of sweet things. She ate half a bag of cookies, coolly, standing there. "Shouldn't we go easy?" you asked. "Won't they mind?"

"Who's they?" she said.

She and her mother were both named Lily. Everyone called the mother Big Lily, and the daughter was Lily Joyce.

Big Lily ran a factory, which was somewhere else on the property. Big Lily owned so many acres that the factory was invisible; you never saw it. You never knew what it made either—something invented by Lily Joyce's father. She didn't talk about him, except to tell you once that he had shot himself ten years ago and that's when her mother had taken over the company.

Later the two of you went swimming in the pool—you in one of Big Lily's bathing suits, which, embarrassingly, fit you; Lily Joyce in a small white bikini. Chlorinated steam wafted up from the water; the air was hot and murky and stinging, and the light was thick and green. The young man came in and watched you and Lily Joyce swimming for a while. Then he pulled off his shirt and jumped into the water. He teased Lily Joyce and chased her and picked her up and threw her toward the deep end. She came down screaming, splashing, flailing to get away from him. He threatened to pull down her bikini top, and she laughed and laughed.

The next year Big Lily married him. He was twenty-two; Big Lily was forty-seven.

"What's it like to have him as a stepfather?" you asked.

"It's okay," Lily Joyce said, with no expression on her face.

THE MATH TEACHER

He was brusque, but also enthusiastic. He came to class every morning with wet hair, but it never dried, so maybe it was oiled. You could see the neat trails of the comb in it, like ski tracks in the snow. Sometimes in the winter, when you went for a walk in the afternoon—the boys were at sports, but there was nothing for the girls to do between lunch and afternoon study hall—you saw him skiing in the woods. He raised his ski pole to show he had seen you, a salute, and then went on, churning and sliding away under the fir trees.

He was German, or Scandinavian: pragmatic, blue-eyed. He had a crisp energetic encouraging way about him. You liked him but felt guilty around him; he seemed to think better of you than he should have.

In class, he—Mr. Sturm—wrote big columns of numbers on the blackboard, underlining the answers and the equal signs so hard that the chalk squeaked. Then "There!" he would say, turning away from the board toward the class. "Everybody get it?"

Nobody did, but no one said anything.

"Any questions?"

There weren't.

HIS WIFE

She wore her black hair piled on top of her head, a lofty, delicate structure composed of many soft, elaborate little puffs. A croquembouche, you realized years later, coming upon a picture of one in a magazine and instantly thinking of her. All of her was like that—something confected in a bakery. She smelled sweet, her white skin was powdered, her nails were tapered and polished pale pink; when she raised her finger in the classroom, you could see the sun shining pinkly through her fingertip.

You were nervous around her at first, because you started in the school at mid-year and you had never studied a foreign language before. In class the first day she said something to you in Spanish, which you didn't understand. Then she asked you in English to conjugate the verb *"decir."* You sat there while she smiled encouragingly, and finally you said that you didn't know what *"decir"* meant, and you didn't know what "conjugate" meant. The boys laughed. She swiftly told them, "You may not realize it, but you are being cruel and ignorant." You were grateful for, but embarrassed by, this; it felt like too fervent a defense, too much championing over too little a thing.

She started meeting with you in the afternoons to give you a crash course. Once you got the hang of it, you loved Spanish, memorizing lists of verbs, showing off to her what you'd learned since the last time. ". . . *viviremos, viviréis, vivirán,"* you would finish triumphantly, and she would say, *"Muy bien, Marisol!"* "Marisol" had nothing to do with your real name—a dull, one-syllable thud of a name, you thought—but you had chosen it from the list of Spanish girls' names she'd showed you on your first afternoon with her. "Don't I have to pick one that's sort of the Spanish version of my name?" you had asked.

"Why? Pick a name you wish your parents had given you," she said—and so became something else you'd always wished for, a kind of godmother. A woman who was not your mother, or an aunt, or one of your mother's vaguely impatient friends. A woman who paid attention to you as a *girl*. Your mother

• • •

cared about different things: books, politics. "You can be anything," your mother told you fiercely; and you believed her—with an amendment, also fierce but too humiliating to be said aloud: You could be anything, except pretty. You didn't know how. Hair, skin, nails, clothes—yours were terrible, or at least inept. In those afternoons at Mrs. Sturm's house, you saw things—ruffles, rose-colored lipstick, a fur collar, a charm bracelet shifting and twinkling on a delicate wrist bone—that you didn't see at home, and certainly were not going to see anywhere else at the boys' school. You learned that prettiness was a possible thing to care about, even if you didn't have any idea how to achieve it.

Still, even as you yearned for it, you worried that it was, in fact, trivial—that she might be trivial. In class, she would write on the blackboard, in her big, airy script, *"Las noticias de España."* You knew, from headlines on the front page of *The New York Times,* which was always lying around in your house, that there was actually news from Spain that year: Franco's death, elections, uncertainty about the new king's allegiances. Mrs. Sturm's news was news of nothing, news of fluff. *"Esta semana es Las Fallas,"* she would write, and you would dutifully copy it down, imitating the curly tips of her capital *E* and the way she had of writing *a*'s like the *a*'s in printed books, fat little structures with curving roofs. She explained, glowing with gentle excitement, that the festival of Las Fallas involved the building and burning of large puppets! It was very festive! Perhaps someday you would all go to Valencia and see this for yourselves! Her news was full of festivals—this one was a mass-participation drum festival, that one was a reenactment of a battle between Moors and Christians, fought over a papier-mâché castle. Constant bullfights, lots of flamenco—but sometimes there were special bullfights and special dances—La Feria de Sevilla!

"Olé!" she said, standing at the blackboard, stamping her little heels, lifting her hands still holding the chalk in a graceful dancer's pose. The boys snickered, more than they would have dared to with a teacher who intimidated them but not as much as they would have with a teacher they disliked.

You didn't snicker, but you were embarrassed for her—the nakedness of her fantasy of herself as a fiery señorita. You wanted to protect her. *Look at me!* she seemed to be crowing, innocently, like a naked child darting into the living room during a dinner party. You wanted to wrap her in a blanket and gently lead her out of the room.

After a couple of months you didn't need extra help with Spanish anymore. You'd caught up with the boys, and you were doing well in class. But you kept going to Mrs. Sturm's house: she started having you and Lily Joyce over on Monday afternoons. "We women have to stick together," she said.

She gave you tea in translucent flowered cups, along with cookies that, like everything of Mrs. Sturm's, were small elusive feminine mysteries. What did they taste of? Lemon? Vanilla? Something pale and delicate. Something far removed from the hunky chocolate things you and Lily Joyce tore into together standing in Big Lily's crammed dark pantry.

THE BOYS

There were so many of them. All those heavy shoes clomping down the stairs and along the corridors between classes, all those tweed sport coats. During morning chapel, sitting there with your head bowed as the school chaplain said prayerful things in a stagey voice, you thought: There are two hundred and twenty-seven penises in this room.

• • •

TRYING TO DESCRIBE IT

You couldn't. One weekend you were invited to a slumber party in the town you had moved away from earlier that year, where you'd gone to a regular public school. That night, when you were all sitting around in your pajamas, the girls—your old friends—asked you what it was like to go to school with all those boys.

"It's fine," you said.

"You must be so popular!"

"I guess," you said.

"Do you just kind of . . . have your pick?"

"Well," you said. "It doesn't really work that way." You tried to explain that being one of only two girls made you conspicuous. It made boys not want to be seen talking to you. They were afraid of being teased. They didn't want to stand out, to be different. In a way this was true. But in another way you knew, even as you were saying it, that it was wise-sounding bullshit. Nobody minded being seen talking to Lily Joyce. The boys kidded her, exchanged loud insults with her in the halls, grabbed her green book bag and tossed it to one another over her head as she ran back and forth with her arms waving, trying ineffectually to retrieve it; they imitated her shrieks—"Aaaaah! Aaaaah! Waaah. I'll tell! I'll *tell!*"—and she laughed at the imitations while continuing to shriek that she *would* tell.

Lily Joyce was a small, cute, flirty girl. You were tall, heavy, serious—somehow not a girl at all. You were conspicuous but invisible. The boys who spoke to you asked how you had done on the math test, or if you understood this whole diagramming-sentences thing.

You couldn't tell this to your old friends. What's wrong

with me? you thought, and tried not to think, all the time. You worried that there was some fundamental thing that might be missing, some difference between you and other girls that was just now starting to show itself but that would become more and more apparent as you grew up, like the progressive divergence of two nearly parallel, but not parallel, lines.

VON BRUYLING

Once, though, a boy did say something to you.

"Any time you want it, I can give it to you."

He was older, a ninth-grader (the school went up only through ninth grade), someone whose voice had changed, who shaved. He said it to you in a low voice, coming up behind you on the stairs and smoothly passing you before you were sure you'd actually heard him.

But you did hear him. His name was von Bruyling. You hadn't liked him, even before he muttered to you on the stairs—he wasn't nice, he wasn't smart. You got that what he'd said had been a joke. A mean joke. You, he was implying, were the last person who would ever want it, and the last person he'd ever want to give it to.

Still, sometimes after that when you were home lying on your bed, with the door shut and your hand between your legs, you thought of von Bruyling's stupid face, and his low voice growling those words over and over.

THE STRING BASS

Another embarrassment: to play an instrument that looked like you. They'd assigned it to you, or you to it, in your old public school, because you were tall and strong and could physically handle it. Now you were stuck with it. String bass players were rare, so you'd won a scholarship to take lessons at a conservatory. Your mother, almost maniacally proud of what she had decided must be prodigious musical talent, drove you there every Saturday. The string bass lay across the backseat, its neck and scroll sticking out through the open car window; you wished for a tree growing a little too close to the road, or the sudden press of a tunnel wall. The bass decapitated; you and your mother safe; but your mother somehow knocked sensible, agreeing to let you quit.

Your bass teacher loathed you for loathing the instrument. Every lesson was the same: you would plunk out a few notes, and he would stop you. "Did you practice?"

"Some," you would say.

"You have to practice."

"I know."

Practicing was the most boring thing you had ever done. Plunk plunk plunk (rest). Plunk plunk plunk (rest). That was pretty much how the string-bass part went in every piece of music your teacher assigned you. He was right, you never practiced.

Then one afternoon at school, a boy came up to you and said, "I hear you play the bass."

"Yeah," you said, wary. You weren't expecting another von Bruyling incident—this kid was younger, and he seemed

65

nice—but you had found that in this school humiliation lurked everywhere and jumped out when you forgot to look for it.

"Because I'm putting together a rock band," the boy, whose name was Henderson, went on.

So then you were the bass player in a rock band.

During the whole time you were in it, the band played only one number, over and over, a song called "Groovin' with Mr. Bloe"—which, in turn, at least the way your band played it, had only one phrase of music, repeated over and over. The bass part went: plunk plunk-plunk-plunk, plunk-plunk-plunk, plunk-plunk-plunk plunk; and so could not claim to be much more interesting than the bass parts your conservatory teacher assigned you. But playing in a rock band felt strange and glamorous, out of character for you. Upstairs in your room you practiced "Groovin' with Mr. Bloe" with a diligence and fastidious musicality that would have made your conservatory teacher cry if he had ever had the chance to see it.

After a few weeks you made up your own words to "Mr. Bloe"—an incantation for Henderson to fall in love with you—and sang them softly in your room while you practiced, and silently whenever you played with the band.

TELLING

Eventually you told Lily Joyce. "Huh," she said. "Henderson?" She'd been waiting a long time for you to start liking a boy. In the time you'd known her she'd liked Stewart, Cook, Childs, McDonald, Chesborough, Hilts, and Sperber. They were all boarders at the school; they would get off-campus permissions to go to her house on Saturdays, mostly one at a time, but Chesborough and Hilts she invited together, because she liked them both.

"What do you do when they come over?" you had asked her once.

Lily Joyce shrugged. "Swim. Listen to records. Sometimes we make out." With Chesborough she had played something called Seven Minutes in Heaven. You didn't know what it was, and you didn't ask Lily Joyce to explain. But Chesborough was another one of those manlike, shaving ninth-graders; and Lily Joyce's exact words were "I let him play Seven Minutes in Heaven," so you sort of knew.

"Why Henderson?" she asked you.

You weren't going to give Lily Joyce a list of reasons. *He's so clean. I like how his eyes are blue and his eyelashes are dark. I even like how his glasses are held together on one side with tape. He's a very serious, not very good guitarist.* You didn't like him because of those things; it was more that you liked those things because you liked him. "He's cute," you told Lily Joyce.

This was a term she recognized and honored: it was valid currency with her. "What are you going to do?" she asked.

"Do?"

"I know. You need to get Mrs. Sturm to put you with him at the dance."

There are children who are too old to be children. It stops being a problem when they get older—they grow into themselves—but before that happens it's perpetually awkward. For you it was a mix of judgment and wistfulness. You thought all this stuff was stupid, but you also had no idea how to get it, and you wanted it.

"Oh, goody. Let's," you said to Lily Joyce. She laughed; she liked it when you were sarcastic. Egged on, you grabbed her hand and started skipping toward the Sturms' house. The two of you skipped along the colonnade, laughing, just as the boys were trailing out of their dorms to go down to the gym for sports. You felt wildly happy, bounding forward with the wind blowing against your face and hair, with all those boys watching. (Later, though, you'd use the memory to humiliate yourself: it had felt like two pretty girls skipping along a colonnade, but it must have looked like big you galumphing along beside little Lily Joyce.)

Mrs. Sturm made tea and put out the mysterious pale cookies on a flowered plate. You sat in her living room, where she always had a fire going on these winter afternoons. "Well, ladies," she said.

"Ask her," said Lily Joyce to you.

"No, that's okay," you said. You knew that Mrs. Sturm was in charge of organizing the upcoming dance, and that each boy from your school would be "put with" a girl bused in from some girls' school. But asking her to put you with Henderson seemed crass to you, dishonorable. She liked you; didn't you owe it to her not to take advantage of that fondness by asking for a special favor? Maybe you would end up with Henderson anyway, either accidentally or because Mrs. Sturm, with her almost magical delicacy, would somehow know without being told to put the two of you together.

Besides, you were afraid to tell her you liked a boy. You didn't want to bore her, or make yourself look silly.

But Lily Joyce was pointing at you. "Mrs. Sturm, she wants to be put with Henderson for the dance, and I want to be with Sperber."

Mrs. Sturm went over to her writing desk—a small, many-compartmented thing that she had told you was an old campaign chest from the time of the Napoleonic wars—and

・ ・ ・

came back with a pad and a tiny pencil. "Lily Joyce, Jeff Sperber," she said, writing. She smiled at Lily Joyce, and then at you.
"And Mark Henderson?"

You nodded, emboldened by her matter-of-fact feminine
complicity: all right, you would throw yourself onto the con-
veyor belt and let it carry you toward the dance.

"Mark Henderson," she said in her light, silvery voice as she
wrote. "Very sweet boy." She smiled at you again. "*Muy bien,
Marisol.*"

AT THE DANCE

Your band played. You were up on a platform, grooving with
Mr. Bloe. Then suddenly Henderson lifted his head and yelled
out, "Drum solo!" and the kid on drums went crazy for a few
minutes, banging out what sounded like a big collision of pots
and pans and sandpaper all happening in a bowling alley. "Key-
board!" yelled Henderson, and you started to realize that you
were going to be next. Shit. "Bass!" shouted Henderson, and
the other instruments quieted down and there you were—the
lighting didn't change but you felt like it had and that you
were suddenly standing in a cone of merciless brightness—and
you didn't know what to do, but you settled for plunking out
your usual sequence of notes with what you hoped was special
emphasis, as loudly as possible, twice; and then you nodded
at Henderson and he went into his own loud, squealy guitar
solo which, you saw then, had been the whole reason why he'd
accorded solos to the rest of you.

Seeing this—how badly he had wanted to play this energetic, incoherent solo, how transparently he'd tried to hide his
desire to do it, how the tape on his glasses gleamed beneath

the lights—made you tender toward him, and maybe a little less shy when Mr. Bloe finally came to an end and you laid down your instruments and joined the dance. Still, you were pretty shy.

"Mrs. Sturm put us together," Henderson said, leading you over to the punch table.

You shrugged. Mrs. Sturm winked at you from her seat by the refreshment tray.

You and Henderson fast-danced. Then you slow-danced. He held one of your hands and put his other arm around your waist, leaving six inches between you: mannerly, respectful, correct, a relief, disappointing. Everyone else was hugging, barely moving. All these strange girls had arrived on a bus, pretty, in pretty dresses, and had gone in straight for the kill. Their faces were buried in the shoulders of the boys from your school. They were letting themselves be touched, and kissed, forgetting or not caring about the teachers who were chaperoning. Sperber's hands were moving lower on Lily Joyce's back; her dress was hiked up and you could see the striped cotton of her underpants. Mr. Sturm came over and said something to them, and they moved apart a little. The Sturms danced: majestically. They looked like ice skaters. It would have been funny, if they had done it with any less grace or dignity.

In the last slow dance Henderson pulled you gently to his chest and you were one of the hugging couples. "I like you," he said, low against your ear. "You're my girl."

IN YOUR BED

You replayed it over and over. He holds you. "I like you," he says. "You're my girl."

• • •

YOU ARE NORMAL

Or if not quite normal, then at least pretty close.

YOUR GODMOTHER

"I'm so glad for you," Mrs. Sturm said. "Tell me everything."

You did. About how Henderson was getting off-campus permissions now and coming over to your house, often, on Saturday afternoons. How much he liked your parents, and how much they seemed to like him. How your mother cooked for him: pot roast, spaghetti and meatballs, rice pudding—he said her rice pudding was his favorite dessert ever. How he teased your little brother and sister (he introduced himself to them using an outlandish false name, and refused to back away from it even when they shrieked at him to tell them the truth), and how they teased him about his accent (he was from Kentucky). How gentle he was when he petted your old German shepherd. How you and he went for long walks in the fields and woods behind your house, how the two of you never ran out of things to talk about.

"He's a nice boy," Mrs. Sturm said. "A real gentleman."

This was an afternoon when the two of you were alone in front of her fire, an afternoon when you'd just dropped by, hoping to see her. Lily Joyce was home with a cold. You would not have talked this way if she'd been there. You wanted to tell Mrs. Sturm these things about Henderson: she would understand them. Lily Joyce was always trying to pry things out of you, but if you told her she would call it "the sappy stuff" and want more details about the kissing. "Has he tried to put his hand

71

inside your shirt yet?" she would ask, in a voice that was impatient, excited, but also gruff and businesslike: if the answer had been "yes," she would have had an entire set of campaign plans ready to unfurl and explain to you in detail. "Of course not," you said, and you could see her rolling up the plans again and putting them away.

You had talked to Lily Joyce some about the kissing—you had technical questions that you knew she would be able to answer—but you didn't mention it to Mrs. Sturm. It was private; and your conversation with Mrs. Sturm was about something more. You didn't use the word—neither of you did—but you were talking about love.

"When I met my husband," she told you, "I knew right away. I was very young. Not as young as you are, but young. It was my junior year of college, I was spending it in Madrid. He'd finished graduate school—he studied mathematics at Göttingen, did you know that?—and he was backpacking around Europe with a couple of friends. We met standing in line to get into the Prado."

Suddenly you were nervous. You were moved that a grown-up—this grown-up—would talk to you so frankly. But you had never heard of Göttingen or the Prado, didn't want to interrupt to ask what they were, hoped she wouldn't quiz you on them later. And though you dreamed about marrying Henderson, you didn't expect to actually do it. You loved Mrs. Sturm for taking you seriously, but she was taking you too seriously.

"I was intimidated," she said. "He was older. So confident. He had so many languages—German, Spanish, Italian, French, even some Dutch. And so handsome! Unattainable, I thought, when he spoke to me. But he did speak to me. Smitten, he told me later. Right away he was smitten. He told me I was beautiful." She smiled at you, and there was a silence. She wrapped her soft cream-colored shawl more tightly around her shoulders and crossed her arms, hugging herself.

For some reason you expected that now she would say something about children, about how sad it was that she and Mr. Sturm didn't have any. But what she said next surprised you.

"Marry for kindness."

The front door opened and Mr. Sturm walked in.

"Well," Mrs. Sturm said. "This is a surprise." She trailed a white forearm over the back of the sofa, and he came and took her hand.

"Darling," he said, and kissed her forehead. "A pleasant one, I hope."

"We were just talking about you."

"*Sturm und Drang*," he said, and she laughed and so did you. You had heard him make this joke in math class, after he'd assigned an especially tough problem to solve. You could tell from the way she laughed that she had heard the joke before, too, and that she was protecting him from knowing how many times he'd already told it.

MEN

You were getting that men were strong and fragile, powerfully tempting and dangerous, gentle and mean, impressive and obtuse, in need of both placating and protection. Meanwhile the boys' school kept ticking away with its own peculiar, habitual brutality.

The day after spring vacation ended and all the boarders

THE NEWS FROM SPAIN

came back to school, a boy in your English class was crying. He was quietly but audibly sniffling, and his face was red and wet.

"What's the problem, Lederman?" the teacher asked. "*Homesick?*"

The boy didn't answer. The teacher stood up, came out swiftly from behind his desk, grabbed the back of Lederman's blazer, and lifted him into the air. He carried Lederman— a small boy; he dangled like a kitten—to the door, opened it, and threw him out into the hall.

"Stay there until you're ready to start acting like a man."

No one spoke to Lederman after class, when the bell rang and he came back into the classroom with his head down to collect his book bag, so you didn't either.

There was a prayer you all said in morning chapel, right after the Lord's Prayer. It started with *Dear Lord in your wisdom guide my steps,* and it ended: *Make me strong and sound and more a man each day.*

THE NEWS

One morning in Spanish Mrs. Sturm fainted. She was in the middle of *las noticias,* talking about one of her innocent, rustic, pinkly romantic festivals—something about bulls, as usual, bulls and flowers—when she suddenly said, "Oh," and then folded sideways and slid to the floor.

Several of the boys jumped up and ran to her. They stood around; they knelt; one boy very lightly patted her shoulder. "Mrs. Sturm," he said. "Um, Mrs. Sturm."

You got up and went over too. "What should we do?" the boys were saying.

Her eyelids flickered, and she made a series of soft, mewing little moans. "Oh . . . oh . . . oh." She tried to sit up. "Oh . . . ," and her head sank down again.

You didn't try to help. You loved her, she'd been so good to you; but watching her lying on the floor, you felt no alarm, no sympathy. Only a cold disapproval at the whole performance. That's what it seemed like to you: a performance. The graceful slump to the floor, the bewildered fluttery coming-to amid a group of worried, gallant males—this was one of your own secret fantasies for yourself. You would faint, Henderson would catch you, bend over you, revive you. You had imagined it, but you would never actually permit it to happen. You felt, austerely, that she could have chosen not to faint. You thought this sort of thing was controllable. You recognized this scene and deplored it. She was a grown-up; she should have known better.

Two of the boys helped her to sit up, supporting her shoulders with surprisingly competent and unafraid solicitude. Someone ran to get help from the front office. "I'm all right, I'm all right," she kept murmuring. You saw that her hair was coming down: the structure had toppled, not all the way, but it was listing, and some of the little puffs were unwinding and sticking out in tufts from her head. That's when you recovered your tenderness for her, and your love; and you pitied her.

The next day the science teacher taught math; and the assistant headmaster sat in the classroom during Spanish while you all did exercises out of the textbook. Mrs. Sturm was sick, you thought, and Mr. Sturm must be taking care of her. You were coming down the stairs to go to lunch when Lily Joyce grabbed you by the arm and pulled you into the ladies' room. "Did you hear about the Sturms?"

"Are they having a baby?" you asked, with a sudden wild lift of joy. That would fix everything, you thought, without beginning to think yet about what it was that needed fixing.

"No, no," Lily Joyce panted. "She's been sleeping with the boys."

"What boys?" you asked stupidly. You honestly didn't understand what she meant.

Lily Joyce lifted her arm and made a big circling gesture that seemed to encompass the entire school. "*These* boys. I don't know who all of them are yet, but . . . ," and she mentioned a few names, mostly boys you knew by sight but had never spoken to. Then ". . . and von Bruyling," she said.

"That's disgusting," you said; but all of a sudden you believed her.

"She's fired," Lily Joyce whispered, unlocking the ladies' room door—you would both have to run, if you didn't want to be marked down in conduct for being late to lunch—"and he quit. They're leaving."

WHAT YOU SAW

Early the next morning, when your mother drove you to school, the Sturms' pale blue station wagon was turning out of the main driveway as your car slowed to turn in. You saw that the car was packed full with their things. He must have been driving, but you didn't see him. What you saw, in the quick blur of their car turning away from yours, was her drooping head resting on her hand, and her pale forearm propped against the window.

• • •

THE REST OF THE STORY

You never knew it. Not all of it. But you got some pieces over the years.

You heard more names, of more boys. Some were big muscled football players; some were small and childlike and scholarly. There was no pattern.

You heard that Mr. Sturm had hanged himself. You had no way of knowing if it was true. You remembered him coming home unexpectedly that afternoon when you and Mrs. Sturm had been talking, and you wondered if he'd been trying to catch her with a boy, or trying to prevent her from doing something she couldn't stop herself from doing.

You thought of her saying, "Marry for kindness."

You graduated from the boys' school and went on to another school, where you were happier.

You heard that Big Lily had come home from the factory one day and found the young blond man—her husband—in bed with some girl, had thrown him out, had cracked up and spent time in a sanitarium, had come home and gone back to running the factory and a number of local charities as well. You heard that Lily Joyce dropped out of high school and married a gas station attendant and moved out west.

You got a letter from Mark Henderson, followed by a visit. You were both seniors, at different boarding schools. He came to see you one Sunday and took you out for a drive. "I need to tell you something," he said. "I feel really bad about this. I need to get it off my chest. I used you."

You laughed. "For what?" Those careful little kisses?

"To get to a home," he said. "I was so homesick. I wanted to eat with a family, around a table."

"That's all right," you said. "You don't need to apologize."

"Yes, I do," he said. "I shouldn't have done it. I shouldn't have acted like I really liked you when really I was just using you."

"It was years ago," you said. "You were a child. Don't worry about it."

Then he asked if you were seeing anyone. "Sort of," you hedged. You weren't, but you were afraid he might ask if you were interested in him.

"*I'm* seeing someone," he said. "A woman." Then he said, "She's a teacher. My dorm mistress, in fact. We joke about that."

So you wondered, then, though the idea of him and Mrs. Sturm had never occurred to you before.

Many years later you heard he was back in Kentucky, working as a high school teacher. You wondered about that too.

THE END

You went to Madrid with your husband. You were in your forties. You stood in line with him at the Prado, and for the first time in years you remembered the Sturms. You told your husband. "What a terrible story," he said. He was holding your hand.

While you waited you looked around at the people standing in line with you. Parents with children, nuns, old men, a group of students shoving one another and laughing, all wearing the same blue cap. You saw beautiful women and smitten men. You thought about how lovers, or any two who fascinate each other, choose in rapture and ignorance.

The line moved and you and your husband moved with it, slowly, toward the old building, where the people who'd waited longest were disappearing, being swallowed into its shadowy mouth.

The News from Spain

This is why she can't sleep. Asleep, dreaming, she's moving. She runs down a street, comically, with no sound, chasing a car that has no driver. It's in Paris, she thinks—or doesn't think, she knows: in dreams you just know. Her feet barely touch the ground, just tap it every now and then, to launch her, floating, into the air. As a child, at the lake in the summer, she used to propel herself through chest-high water this way, leaping softly from pointed toe to pointed toe, great soft arching leaps anchored by the briefest contact with the sandy lake bottom.

What would she do, in this dream, if she caught up with the car? That's not the point. The car is there to lead her through the streets, a benevolent conductor. *This way,* it says. *Now this way.* Her legs, her feet, her toes, follow it without thinking, easily, an ease she doesn't register in the dream.

But it's the ease that pierces her when she wakes up. The

unnoticed, taken-for-granted ease, of muscles doing what she has told them—unaware of telling them—to do. Waking, her eyes are slitted, hot, leaking; her face is wet. The feeling of loss, of having something dangled and then taken away, is terrible. So is the self-pity, and the sense of danger. She spent a long time feeling sorry for herself, before she finally shoved all that aside. Even the smallest taste of that, now, the most delicate exploratory lick, feels dangerous, repulsive. Whatever you do, don't go back there again.

In the early days, she used to think: Just give me five more minutes of movement. Not even dancing—just running, walking. Or not even that. I'd settle for a voluntary shift, a decision and then the tiniest action, to move a leg an inch, to shake a wrinkle out of a trouser leg. Just let me do that once more, and then I won't ask for anything else. It was like a bereavement—she'd felt this way after the death of her grandmother. Just let me see her one more time, and that will be enough. You imagined that a brief restoration, granted with full knowledge of the overall permanence of the loss, would be sweet: the scratch that would make the itch stop itching. But no, she saw, each time she woke from one of these vivid, utterly convincing dreams. The itch just itched more.

So she can't sleep. There are pills, big, red, slippery. They deliver something that is not really sleep—it's grimmer, more bureaucratic, doled out reliably regardless of individual circumstances. It's mere unconsciousness, an ellipsis in time. But it's dreamless. Every few nights, frantic and grumpy with fatigue, she asks her husband for a pill. "I need to be clonked on the head with the sledgehammer," she says, and he smiles kindly at her and goes into the bathroom. He sits with her while they wait for the pill to work. She thinks he would feel it ungallant not to, though on the nights when she doesn't take a pill she

• • • •

is alone in this room, struggling to sleep and struggling not to sleep. His bed is in the small room opposite the kitchen at the end of the hall. Decades ago, before their apartment was divided from several others that would have made up its original, generous sprawl, it had been a maid's room. She and her husband have always called it "the den"—the earnestly rugged American idiom a delight to him.

(Biographers, early in the next century, forty years from now, will write about this little room, speculating on whether he was already sleeping there before she got sick, suggesting that the marriage was already in trouble, that they were on the brink of separating, that he stayed on after her illness out of a sense of duty and guilt—but he and she will both be dead by the time these rumors become public. She, herself, would not have been able to answer this question, except to remark that nothing was as clear-cut as that, either in their marriage or in any marriage, or in anything, for that matter. Sometimes before she got sick he'd slept in the den, saying he'd been working late and hadn't wanted to disturb her. Sometimes he'd slept there with no comment. Sometimes he'd slept in the bedroom with her. Sometimes *she'd* slept in the den, either for the hell of it or because his snoring had awakened her in the night and she'd pulled the quilt from the foot of their bed and wandered down the hall—wandered! Such a vague, careless word, but still an active verb, an action that required volition and neurons and muscles to work together busily and efficiently, even while you were prodigally unaware of them—to sleep, in happy, self-righteous silence, alone.)

Now her husband sits in the orange tweed armchair beside her bed while they wait for tonight's pill to embrace her and pull her down. The water glass, half empty, is on the bedside table. The lamps are turned off. The pillows are in their right places, behind her neck and shoulders. "It's like leaving on a trip," she tells him. "When you're on the boat and the luggage is all there too, and the guests have gone ashore. The responsibilities are all done—you just have to relax and wait for the boat to pull away from the pier."

"And drink champagne," her husband says.

"That's right, you have to drink champagne."

"So you do still have responsibilities."

She smiles. "Poor you."

Speaking of boats—and maybe this is why she did—he is sailing tomorrow, on the *France,* taking the company on a six-week tour. She misses touring, misses Europe, misses going alone with him to museums and odd corners of cities and small, cheerful restaurants for late-night suppers. That private, small, lighted world you could find for yourselves in the midst of traveling. She misses, too, being in groups with him: being one of many in company class, or rehearsal, or at a large, crazy party given by some rich admirer in the lantern-lit garden of a villa—Fiesole, Neuilly—seeing him at a distance, his calm formality, knowing that she was the one who would be alone with him, behind a locked door, at the end of the night. Knowing it but never quite believing it was true. Running down a street, jumping with him into a taxi. "The getaway car," he would say.

She has learned, with this sort of perilous reminiscence, how to turn it off, like a faucet. Stop it the minute you notice it's beginning to drip. Close the pipes.

"Did you eat?" she asks.

"Not yet. I will." He sounds tired.

"Malcolm made macaroni."

"Ah. Try to say it three times fast," he says instantly, always that quick exhilaration at being able to make a joke that is

• • • •

American, to play with Americanisms as nimbly as a cat batting a ball of yarn.

They talk more, about the itinerary, about who is scheduled to come in to help her when. An unnecessary conversation—everything is efficiently arranged, as always; she is never left alone for too long; and in an extreme emergency she'd be capable of dragging herself to the telephone—but, thinking that he is reassuring her, it makes him feel better to have it. "I know," she says. And: "Yes, that's right."

She's beginning to get sleepy now—just a hint of it, the first promise of more to come. It's slow, luxurious. He hears it in her voice; and she hears the relief in his.

"So would you like a story?"

"Yes," she says.

He leans back in his chair, lifts his chin, and taps his lips with his fingertips, thinking. The stories he tells her are old Russian ones, tales so embedded in his childhood he can't remember learning them—from his mother? A teacher? An old book in the Maryinsky schoolroom? They are like songs; he tells them the same way each time, almost in the same words but not quite: he still hears them in Russian, and translates as he speaks. Witches, forests, horsemen, fools. Beautiful maidens. Talking wolves and roosters. Brave tsarinas. Clever devils whose human victims prove, wryly, to be even cleverer. Soldiers whose mettle is tested through nights full of shrieking demons. Cities turned to stone.

"One night," he begins now, "there was a soldier who had too much to drink . . ."

"Oh, this one. We had this one last week."

"No, this is different soldier. All soldiers are drunk." He thinks for a moment. "That is why only few die in duels." He stands up, staggering and reeling. Paces away from her, whirls to face the foot of her bed, points an unsteady finger in her direction, and jerks his arm, miming a pistol shot that even she—drugged, in near darkness—can tell would have missed wildly.

"Who will I find to be this silly with me when you're away?" she murmurs, before she can stop herself.

He sits again and takes hold of her hand for a moment, very lightly, before letting go and folding his arms across his chest. "One night there was a soldier who had too much to drink."

She nods. He begins to tell her about the soldier, words she will not remember the next morning. Sleep comes, an abrupt and opaque curtain dropping.

In the morning, there's the leave-taking. A lot of bustle, which she hates. Just go. But she keeps her face placid, good-humored; she sits tucked in her wheelchair by the living room windows, where the sun turns the leaves of the plants pale and bright and translucent. He has the passport, the handkerchiefs. His luggage is ready. The parquet creaks under his hurrying feet. He will send her telegrams and letters. "Yes, yes," she says, grinning at him.

"And you two will be all right?" he says, meaning her and the cat.

"We're planning to get into trouble, preferably involving the police, as soon as you leave."

Finally he bends to embrace her, and she lifts her arms to him. They kiss—familiar, fond, nothing more, except she thinks there is a kind of careful brightness between them, an

. . . .

implicit understanding that to regret, or even acknowledge any awareness of, their mutual unerotic kindness would be pointless and unwise. Malcolm has tactfully and unnecessarily left the room. "Bye, cutie," she says against her husband's rough warm neck.

She would never have used a word like that—a condescending endearment, or indeed any endearment—before she got sick.

2

Malcolm knows when not to talk. He knows when she's tired, when bright conversation would evoke from her an automatic, well-mannered, equal, even superior brightness that would ultimately make her even more tired. He knows when solicitude would annoy or sadden her, would hit her as infantilizing. He knows when there is nothing to say. She has never told him that his ability to be silent is one of the things she likes about him, but he knows it is. She can be scorching about some of the other aides-de-carcass (her term): Miss Soap Opera, Fräulein Sacher-Masoch, The Blinding Blond, Chatty Ballet Man (who was fired after saying "Ah, the ballet, the ballet"). The nicknames were sharp but not mean; mostly she liked these people, she was even grateful to them, but she needed to blow off steam. "You know what I call you behind your back?" she asked Malcolm once.

"What?" He wasn't alarmed by her question, though it had never occurred to him to wonder about this.

"Malcolm," she said. Then she said: "What's hardest is to be at such close quarters, always. I miss being alone. You make me feel like I'm alone." She smiled at him. She had a radiant, exciting smile, sophisticated, he thought, mysterious, but also wildly free and childlike—there were more things going on in her face when she smiled than in any other face he'd ever seen—and he had to look away from her in that moment to keep from smothering her with some soulful compliment; he was in danger of turning into Chatty Ballet Man.

This morning, once her husband has left, Malcolm sees that she wants to be quiet but busy. She wheels her chair into the den to sort through the mail. Malcolm follows. He leans down to put one arm around her shoulders and the other beneath her knees, lifts her briefly out of the chair and onto the narrow, unmade bed, steadies her while he fits a hard cushion into the seat of the wheelchair, then tucks his arm under her knees again and swings her back into the chair. He puts another cushion under her feet. Now she is raised to the right height for working at the desk. She is silent and relaxed, very still, as he accomplishes this operation.

He would never say aloud (the ghost of Chatty Ballet Man again) that it's like partnering, but he has thought it, that kind of mute, aloof acceptance of the boy's support. But it can be messy, awkward, not like partnering at all, her disciplined, carefully placed arms belonging to an entirely different creature from the dangling legs—a greyhound ending in a scarecrow, he has thought. Or: a mermaid stranded on land.

You could make a ballet about paralysis—her husband did once, years ago, long before she got sick, when she was still almost a child. She danced, ran all over the stage, was stricken, and then sat in a wheelchair. It was a small piece, done for charity, performed once. Years before he knew her, or even came to New York, Malcolm happened to read the review of that ballet, sitting in the periodicals room of the newly integrated but still

• • • •

nerve-racking public library in the Kentucky town where he grew up. He used to go there on Saturdays to read *The New York Times*—the news but mostly the arts section, the movie and dance reviews—while the two librarians passed by to see how he was doing, the one who ostentatiously smiled to show he was welcome and the one who didn't. He remembers that review, for some reason; it talked about the beauty of her arms and what she did with her upper body as she sat in the wheelchair. Someone—well, Tim, who is in the company—has told Malcolm her husband can't bear to remember that he put her in that piece.

Once she is settled, Malcolm hands her the fine silver knife she uses to slit open the envelopes, positions the wastebasket next to her chair, and goes into the kitchen to get the coffee, which he and she both like to drink all through the morning, very strong, with cream. He carries it in to her on a tray, cup and saucer and a blue-and-white Danish coffeepot, delicate and easy to lift but large so that she'll be well supplied and won't have to call for more. Unlike the physical things he does for her body, which are not unmentionable but which go unmentioned—they happen in some different world that contains only facts, necessities, mechanics—this gracefully civilized bit of service evokes her soft, pleasant "Thank you," and one of those radiant smiles.

Then—he is stripping the sheets from the bed, she has gone back to the mail—she says, "Oh, God." She is looking at an envelope. From where Malcolm is standing, a few feet away, he recognizes her husband's scrawly black handwriting.

"What?"

"Wait," she says. She slices open the envelope, scans the letter and laughs, a small, sour, exasperated sigh of a laugh. She holds the white sheet of stationery out to Malcolm.

87

Dear Sweetheart—

I am in a taxicab going down to the dock, or I am on the dock, or already on the boat as you read this. Crowded, noisy, loud horns, people say good-bye and they love each other. Even though none of this has happened yet, it will, and I will miss you. Be good and careful and eat well, not too much though, and I will come home to you soon.

Love—

Malcolm nods, looks at her, and waits. It seems, to him, like a nice letter; but what matters is how it seems to her.

"What do you think?" she asks, in an overly bright, impatient, baiting voice. She's smiling. *Tell me,* she invites. *Tell me, and I'll tell you you're wrong.*

He shakes his head.

She laughs and ducks her head, a graceful little bow, acknowledging his prudence. "Well," she says, "it's what you do with a child. You write the stack of letters before you go away, and you give them to a family friend to mail. One a day, or every other day; some prearranged schedule. That way, the child thinks you are thinking of her, and you can go off and be out of reach without worrying that she's feeling neglected."

Wouldn't that be a good thing? he wonders. The notion that someone might take so much trouble to console and please a child is new to him. Best, maybe, to be adored with passion, as a lover; but if you couldn't have that, then wasn't the next best thing to be a child beloved enough to inspire such elaborate contrivance?

"You're quick," is what he says. "Right, he must have mailed it several days ago."

"I'm crazy, is what you mean. To be already convinced that

• • • •

this is only the first of these letters, that there will be more. As they say in mystery novels." He must look baffled (he is), because she adds, "In Agatha Christie, whenever a threatening note arrives, someone says, 'This is only the first.' "

"This is a threatening note?"

"Malcolm, don't be stupid." Her voice is gentle. He sees that she is close to tears. Well, of course she is. Her husband is in love with someone else.

"Malcolm," she says, "you're not the one mailing them, are you? He didn't give them to you?"

"No," he says, startled, truthful.

"Oh, good. That really would be more than I could stand." She reaches for his hand and, without looking at him, leans her cheek very briefly against his wrist.

There's been a long string of these girls. She was one of them. She had predecessors—some wives, some not—and she's had successors.

Sitting here, sorting the bills (her husband used to insist on doing them until she finally told him it was ridiculous, she was sitting around twiddling her thumbs so much that her entire brain felt twiddly, and just give her please the goddamn bills), anticipating lunch, she's thinking about them, this string of women, and trying to remember how she thought about it all when she was the new one. Not even yet the new one—but the upcoming one, the future one, the one beginning to be singled out. None of it had happened yet, but she could tell that the light was shining on her, flickering sometimes but getting stronger as she got closer to it. All she had to do was walk toward it; and it shone, invitingly, approving of the way she walked.

She was young and dumb, she thinks now. Ruthless. No,

young. Trusting the grown-ups, and he was the leader of the grown-ups. She had not seen anyone acting upset—his wife continued to be as kind as ever—and, not seeing any hurt, it had incredibly not occurred to her that she was part of something hurtful. Everyone seemed to feel *Oh, yes, of course;* so she felt it too.

If it hadn't been you, it would have been someone else, an older dancer said to her—such a nonchalant blend of malice and reassurance, though at the time she'd missed the malice and had not needed to be reassured.

Oh, well, if it hadn't been you, it would have been someone else, she has thought in the years since then, telegraphing her thoughts in the general direction of some new ballerina who was bumbling, pale and blank and fluttery, toward that same bright light.

"Oh, well." It's artifice, a performance, whether said of love or illness, before an audience or just to oneself. No one really thinks "Oh, well," but repeated often enough, rehearsed, it can become admirable, almost believable.

This time, though, she can't say it. She's tried. She's sent tokens—flowers, joke gifts, once a very old Russian cross—on opening nights. She's hosted at dinner a couple of times, evenings that were awkward, painful, not because of her husband's bewitchment but because of the new one's shyness, which is so extreme that it's a kind of encapsulation. She's coined a name for her—he's always liked young dancers, babies, but this one is even younger: "How goes it with the Infant?" she's asked her husband sometimes, with a kind of hearty, almost bawdy cheer that made her shudder. "Infant does very well," he would answer. Look, they can speak of it! They can share a joke!

Only lately, he hasn't spoken or joked about it. "How's the Infant?" "Fine," he says, vaguely, as if he isn't quite sure which

• • • •

infant she's referring to. In the beginning he talked a lot about what the Infant could do—how high, how fast, how bravely. "No fear—none. She's like cat." He's compared other dancers to other things—"She's like knife, clean, bam!" "She's like smoke." "She's like happy little dog—jumps until you pat on the head"—but of the Infant, now, he's gotten quieter. It isn't the silence of having moved on; it's a different silence, of having moved deeper. He is not making new ballets for anyone else, and he's casting the Infant in all the old dances, wanting to see what they'll look like on her. The old dancers are miffed and alarmed and helpless; the young ones cry and try to get thinner. She hears all this, shut up in the apartment. People bring in the gossip along with the books and the flowers. She shrugs. She sees herself shrugging, in the mirror that leans against one of the living room walls, a mirror she uses for physical therapy and otherwise pretty much ignores.

"Oh, dear," said one visitor, who'd been fretting about losing her old parts and was suddenly aware of having been thoughtless. "But I guess there are worse things in life."

"Yes," she said, and laughed, "like frozen spinach. Have you ever tasted it? Somehow I never had, but I got curious last week. Oh, just frighteningly awful." She glanced again at the mirror and saw the two of them laughing, the old chic troubled dancer and herself merrily chortling in her wheelchair, and she felt sick.

Sometimes she looks at Malcolm, and he kicks people out. "She's tired," he says; or he refers to some fictitious imminent appointment. It's like being a Tudor monarch, irrational and absolute: all she has to do is lift a querulous eyebrow, and he dispatches the offender. (Except Tudor monarchs didn't have eyebrows: too fair, or maybe they'd plucked them. She'd gone on a reading binge—all the wives. Which sounds pointed—though at least her husband has never resorted to decapitation—but wasn't, because it was only one of many binges. Russian and French history; Turgenev, Chekhov, Maupassant; Beverley Nichols and then a slew of gardening histories; Lafcadio Hearn; Denton Welch; murder mysteries; Plato, Aeschylus, Virgil; and a lot more, books brought over from the public library or ordered from London or Paris, many cookbooks, volumes of diaries and letters. All the reading she never did when she was young and just danced: a spotty curriculum entirely based on her own happy, avid whims.)

But this morning, with the company safely packed onto the boat, there are no worried, exhausting visitors for her to jolly along. There's the mail, the coffee, the tour of the plants (looking for leaves that might have died since yesterday—there aren't any—and pinching leaves off the geraniums to get the scent), the cat stretched out in a block of sunlight, asleep and grinning, and a Mozart wind serenade on the record player. There's the bathroom stuff; and a shampoo, a long, perilous procedure in which Malcolm binds her with white cloths, mummylike, to a board that slants up to the kitchen sink. Then there's lunch, delicious, a salad with tiny potatoes and thin green beans and olive oil, lemon juice, and salt. And olives. And bread, thickly spread with butter. "Oh, Malcolm, thank you."

She takes her hair out of rollers and brushes it and looks through a cookbook, thinking about dinner. "Haddock stew?" she says to Malcolm, who is folding laundry. The cat sits up and starts energetically washing a leg. "He heard me. Yes, darling, we'll slip you something. You won't starve, I promise."

Then more bathroom stuff and she takes a nap while Malcolm goes out to the fish store and the wine store and the A&P. Then they go out together, she wearing sunglasses and wrapped in a plaid blanket ("my neurasthenic Baden-Baden millionaire outfit," she calls it), and Malcolm pushes her along Riverside Drive, where the wind is cold and the sun breaks the water into tiny blinding smithereens.

She thinks of the boat sliding out of the river this morning. Out of sight of land now. You walk the deck. You rest. You dress for dinner. You have cocktails. You stand by the railing and look at the stars or down at the long foaming triangle of the wake. Nothing appears to be happening, but you're moving slowly toward Europe, and the whole time you are feeling that deep vibrating hum of the engine, without being aware that you feel it.

Malcolm, too, is looking at the river and thinking of the boat.

Of Tim, who may or may not write.

Who offered to let Malcolm stay in his apartment while he was away—an offer that, Malcolm saw, was meant to be generous, but that was actually chilling, since he'd been "staying" there for over a year and had begun at some point to think of himself as living there. Was Tim trying to tell him he was a freeloader? (But Malcolm does buy all the groceries, and cooks as well, on the nights when he isn't working—he always has a meal ready when Tim comes home from the theater.) Or to remind him not to overestimate how close they were, not to make assumptions about the future or even about right now? No, he decided, as Tim went on holding him after speaking, with no sign that any big caution had just been delivered. It was meant warmly. Maybe for Tim it was a step forward, even if to Malcolm it felt like a loss, a sudden discovery that something lovely and unspoken had perhaps not been spoken because it wasn't there.

It would be so good to talk about it, he thinks, looking at

the back of her patterned silk head scarf as he pushes her along the sidewalk. To lay all these messy pieces—hers and his—out on the floor, to turn things this way and that, to speculate. But neither of them would want that conversation. She was too reticent about her marriage, Malcolm didn't want someone else's insights about Tim, they were both exquisitely careful of each other's privacy.

Really, what he would have liked, rather than a solemn dramatic analysis, would have been the freedom to babble about it to someone. To her. She'd be a joy to babble to.

Did you know that Tim isn't short for Timothy? he'd like to say. *His name is actually Timon.*

Of Athens? she'd ask, alert and curious, her mouth curling in that beautiful smile.

No, of Greenwich, Connecticut. They would laugh together. *But I read the play, after I met him. No one reads that play, but I did.*

What did you think?

I don't remember anything about it. Just the title page. I kept flipping back and just looking at that one word on the title page.

No, too sappy. Too confidential. It wouldn't shock her to know that he's mooning over a man (he guesses it wouldn't even surprise her). But he knows that even this kind of talk would be too much, the same way he knew, growing up, sneaking silently out of the house at night, which parts of which floorboards to avoid. She'd be warm and interested. She'd ask questions. Then she'd have to ask more questions, next week, next month. If it went well, she'd have to rejoice. If it ended, she'd have to commiserate. She'd have to be a friend, or do that sprightly false boss-taking-an-interest-in-the-worker business. It would upset their balance, which cannot be explained, but which works.

Maybe he's wrong. Maybe her boredom, which is spectacular, fiendish, at its worst right now—in later years it'll get better; she'll write, teach, travel, regain some actual, rather than just faked, equilibrium—could be helped a little if he were a little less careful with her.

But on the way home what they talk about is the haddock stew. That seductive, engrossing stew! The recipe calls for tomatoes and cream, so, they speculate, it will taste both astringent and sweet. They can start working on it together, if they hurry. He starts running then. The wheelchair rollicks. She screams a little. He will have left by the time it's ready—Fräulein Sacher-Masoch (actually a Scotswoman from Oban, very kind, but with a perpetually terrified expression) is on tonight—but they'll save him some for lunch tomorrow.

3

She's right about the letters. Another comes the next morning, a short, fanciful description of the first day at sea ("captain is pirate, reformed"), and then another each day after that. Funny little made-up stories about people in the company.

This one drank whole bottle of champagne and fell off railing and we had to catch her by the toes as she went over.

That one has mouse in cabin and tried to make friends, but turns out mouse speaks only French and that one never learned it.

They're all postmarked New York, New York. She wonders who is mailing them. Which person did he hand them to and explain what he wanted done with them? She's glad not to know.

The physical therapist comes. The other aides-de-carcass. The maid. A childhood friend. Another friend, a former dancer who became a photographer. Friends who teach, friends whose injuries kept them from the tour, a friend who just had a baby and is trying to get back in shape. The old costume designer, who comes for tea every Friday afternoon, beautifully dressed and made up, bringing brioches. The doctor. The super (the kitchen drain is clogged). Her mother. They are all suspects, except for the childhood friend, who's in for just a week, from Paris. She watches them all, wondering which one is her partner in humiliation.

The only person she shows the letters to is Malcolm. He doesn't say much. She argues with him, trying to make him say that they're horrible. She nags him, she's never spoken to him like this about anything. "Are you being diplomatic, is that it? Or do you really not see?"

"I see that they bother you."

"They're grotesque. They're false."

"Would you like me to just take them when they come, and put them away, before I bring you the mail?"

"God. Don't *you* humor me."

The days go on. She hates this quarreling with him. The more she picks at him the quieter he gets. Silence is one thing when it's spacious, peaceful; but this is something else. She's terrified, she thinks she's marred things between them. She is sure he's gone from liking and admiring her to working for a paycheck. She has to shut up, return to her old reticence. She could, she thinks, if the letters would stop coming.

One day she's railing at him during a procedure for which they both generally stay silent. The letters are insulting, they're condescending, they're a child's toy. They're an indignity.

・　　・　　・　　・

"Oh, so now you want *dignity*?" Malcolm asks. They both look down at what he is doing to her body at that moment; and then, instantly, they both start laughing, the kind of helpless laughter that starts up again every time it seems to be dying down.

4

At home—at Tim's—in the evenings, Malcolm listens to music, reads, and does his exercises, push-ups, sit-ups, dumbbells, and some ballet stretches and warm-ups. He smokes. He eats cereal for dinner. He's waiting.

And then one day he comes home from work, opens the mailbox in the vestibule, and finds a postcard. A picture of the Eiffel Tower.

Got here yesterday. Good food and weather. The schedule is tough. Long wierd days, but no real time to see anything. It's good, though. But I miss New York. T

He carries it upstairs and reads it over and over. Such a relief to have it. How could he have imagined that Tim wouldn't write?

But so little in it. So flat and impersonal. The Eiffel Tower? A sly little joke, or just unoriginal? And "weird" spelled wrong. Tim isn't dumb—how can he sound so dumb?

But missing New York: that's all I need to hear.

Unless he means it literally.

And oh God—the handwriting alone is almost unbearably beautiful.

He props the card against a candlestick on the table in the living room. Looks at it all evening. From far away, pretending to forget that it's there, walking past it and then turning his eyes to catch sudden sight of it again. From up close, holding it in both hands, staring at the bright photograph, the word "PARIS" printed in red at the bottom, as if one might otherwise mistake this for some other Eiffel Tower. Turning it over, again pretending not to have seen it before, pretending he's reading Tim's message for the first time. Relishing the repeated mix of thrill and disappointment—what is it about the disappointment that makes the whole thing somehow lovelier?

When he goes to bed he leaves the card in the living room, leaning against the candlestick. He doesn't need to sleep next to it—he's not that desperate. And this way he can come upon it freshly in the morning.

Over the next few days, he looks at the card so much that he feels like it's fraying. It isn't, really. It's a tough, shiny little piece of manufacturing.

But along with everything else it does to him, it proves that the company has arrived and been on dry land long enough to allow a card to be purchased, written, mailed, and delivered.

A telegram did come for her. "Arrived safely. Paris beautiful of course. Next Turin. Miss you."

But still every day, hating to do it, he brings her mail into the den along with the coffee, and nearly every day, still, there's a letter postmarked from New York. Little fictions about Paris and Turin and Rome.

But she's different, now, about them. "Oh, Malcolm," she says. "It's just getting ridiculous. The poor man."

.   .   .

. . . .

Anyway, she has a project. A reporter called one day, asking if she would agree to an interview. "A major piece, with photographs. The story of your life."

No, thank you, she said. She gets these calls from time to time, and always says no. She hung up the phone. "Someone should write the story of your life," she told the cat. "Now, that would make sensational reading."

"It would," Malcolm said.

"It would scandalize polite society," she went on. "Look at you. You'd have a tale or two to tell, wouldn't you? You'd set the literary world on its ear, if we were to catalog your adventures."

The idea amused both her and Malcolm. All that day, whenever the cat slept (which was most of the time), they described to each other his dreams. When he washed himself, they said, "Big night ahead." When he walked to the kitchen: "Pre-theater snack." By the time Malcolm left, they had devised a tragic love affair for the cat, and when the cat slept the next day, they said, "See? He's taken to his bed."

She starts writing down some of this silliness—little scenarios about the cat, his ambitions and regrets, his amours, puns—on scraps of paper. Malcolm buys her a small notebook to keep next to the bed, so she can fool around with the cat's story when she has trouble sleeping. "You're egging me on," she says.

"Yeah."

Her friend the photographer visits one afternoon. They're all together in the living room, drinking lemonade, when the cat starts suddenly and gallops away down the hall. She shakes her head. "Oh, the press, the press. Is there no escaping the glare of publicity?"

That leads—as she realizes later she hoped it would—to her

telling the photographer about the cat biography, and the photographer saying, "But it needs pictures." And it goes even further: the photographer has a friend in publishing. "Why don't I talk to him? Seriously, what do you think? Would you like me to?"

"Oh, I don't know." Of course she would like it; what's the matter with her? Look how frightened she's become, afraid to admit even to herself that she wants something. "Yes, that would be wonderful," she says.

Two days later, she and the photographer have lunch with the publisher in The Oak Room at The Plaza. Getting there is a big production: Malcolm lifting her into the taxicab, where the photographer steadies her while Malcolm collapses the wheelchair and loads it into the trunk; the two of them wedged on either side of her, holding her upright while the driver maneuvers his cab with that terrified reverence that never fails to amuse her; waiting in the cab as Malcolm carries the wheelchair into the hotel; enduring the conspicuous melodrama of being carried in after it.

"I hope you'll have lunch with us," she said to him earlier. She had thought carefully about how to phrase this. There's no right way. Posing it as a question—*Would you like to join us?*—would have seemed like mere politeness, something said in the hope of being met with refusal. But the other way, the way she said it, has a kind of white-lady or at least noblesse-oblige condescension to it, which she hoped Malcolm would forgive as awkwardness. She would really like him to be at the lunch, but not if being there would make him uncomfortable. So when he did refuse, gently—he said he'd get a hot dog and walk in the park for an hour—she didn't press it.

But now again, in the lobby, as he settles her in the wheelchair, she has the impulse to ask him to stay. She scrambles to think of some therapeutic pretext that might make it easier for him to say yes, but there really isn't one; and the photographer's hands are already reaching out to grasp the handles of the chair, and then the chair is moving across the lush, dizzying carpet, the vast chaotic space, the unfamiliar clamor, so she ends up not saying anything.

Only during lunch, as they're eating their salads, does it register with her that beneath his overcoat he was wearing a suit. She's never seen him in a suit before. He might have put it on just to carry her into this posh lobby, but maybe he was hoping that she would repeat the invitation. She wishes she had. The cat idea is his, too; or at least he is its great champion, and hers. She misses him.

The publisher is a plump, red-faced man who loves the idea. "What a lark! What a lark!" he keeps saying, and she wants to say, *What do you mean, a lark? Get off it, you're not even English;* but she sees that he is nervous—the wheelchair, or whom she's married to, or her old fame, or her perhaps famously rumored reclusiveness, or some combination of these things, or maybe he is just a nervous guy. After lunch he offers her a cigarette (she looks to see if they're Larks, but no, they're Pall Malls), and the three of them sit and smoke and talk business. And then they're out in the lobby again, shaking hands; and Malcolm is there, with his soft reassuring smile; and she's going home in a big Checker taxi, with the promise of a book contract, but even with the excitement she has a momentary pang, remembering how in these cabs she used to love the precarious feeling of riding in the little fold-down jump seat.

5

She asks Malcolm, hesitantly, if he'd be willing to change his hours—to work some nights instead of, or in addition to, the days he's working now. She's having even more than the usual trouble sleeping, and it would make her feel better to have him in sometimes at night, easier than with some of the other aides. "The writing keeps me busy during the day now," she says, "so Miss Soap Opera or the Fräulein, they're fine, I can sort of tune them out. But at night, right now—"

"Sure." Malcolm nods.

He is touched that she would ask him, and happy about the extra money. Since that brief confusing jolt from Tim—*Feel free to stay here while I'm away*—he's been worrying about money, looking at apartment listings in the classifieds, calculating whether he could afford to rent a place of his own, if it came to that. He is soberly aware of the fragility of his qualifications to do reliable, well-paying, interesting work. When things got so fraught with her, a few weeks back, over those letters—of course he could see what was wrong with them, of course he could—he was frozen with fear that saying the wrong thing (sympathizing too little, or sympathizing too much and implicitly criticizing her husband) might cost him his job. If he did lose it, would he be lucky enough to get another one that he loved? And would she ever forgive him, would he see her again? *Sometimes*, he imagines telling her by way of apology, *I am so worried about putting a foot wrong that I'm afraid to put a foot anywhere.*

So now, after they've cooked and had dinner and watched television or listened to music and gotten her into her nightgown, Malcolm sits in the orange tweed armchair next to her bed and they talk. "I figured out who he's in love with," she tells him one night.

"What?" he asks, startled. It's late, after midnight. It's been a rough evening. She's had some pain, which he tried to rub away; and then there was an unscheduled clean-up that required more than a sponge bath, so he had to put her in the contraption (something an aide had rigged up for her in the early days: a beach chair set on a rubber mat in the bathtub, where she sat gripping the rickety metal armrests while you sprayed her with a hose). She is exhausted, and not sleepy, and trying not to take a pill.

"Our boy," she says; and Malcolm relaxes. Oh. The cat. "I know who his femme fatale is."

"Who?"

"Well, it's the Infant's little cat, of course."

He doesn't know what to say.

She goes on. "You've never seen her, have you? Devastating. So innocent and so sleek. Butter wouldn't melt in her mouth. It's no wonder that when he saw her, the thought of every other feline just left his head."

He lets her keep spinning the story. How they met, how they fell in love, how they parted.

But you haven't seen her either, he wants to say. How does she even know the Infant has a cat? Her husband must have mentioned it. Or maybe that was all she and the Infant had found to talk about, those times when the Infant came to dinner. He could weep for this new ingenious, doomed invention, for the frantic, gallant gaiety of it.

She says she's written to her husband about the whole thing—the book, the photographer, the contract. She's gotten a telegram back, congratulating her. Now she's written again to tell him this newest idea, about the Infant's cat. "He'll like that," she tells Malcolm.

There's a silence. "Those letters finally stopped coming," she says.

And he, after a moment, takes a quiet, small risk. "I'm glad."

Another card has come from Tim, from Rome. A picture of the Colosseum. More noncommittal tourist-talk, about the Vatican and the Spanish Steps, and looking forward to getting back to New York.

Malcolm goes through it all again: the initial exalted flaring leap of happiness, the irritation, the analysis, the unease, the longing. He props this card against the other candlestick and sets it next to the Paris one; but then when he walks by and sees them both he says aloud, "Fuck you."

6

Two days later, Malcolm goes down in the morning to check his mail and there's an aerogram. Upstairs, in Tim's apartment, he slits it open carefully so as not to tear the message inside. The thin blue paper is shaking, crackling in his hands. He knows even before he reads it that a sealed message will be different from words written openly on a postcard.

Listen. The tour is wrapping up. Two more nights in Madrid, then Barcelona for three nights, and then back to Paris. What about coming over to meet me? We can have a couple of Paris days (I'll show you the Eiffle Tower) and then figure out where to go from

*there. I have three weeks off and we could have fun. I'll wire money
for a plane ticket. I'll be in Paris again by the time you get this, so
send a telegram to the hotel there and let me know. But I hope you'll
say yes.*

T

He sits at the living room table, holding the letter, not need-
ing to reread it, looking at the familiar, loved room. Faded old
rugs, the long curved sofa with a button-dimpled back, the
old honey-colored chest of drawers that had belonged to Tim's
great-grandmother, the hi-fi cabinet with its shelves of records,
the glass-fronted bookcase filled with Tim's photographs and
Malcolm's books, the blue mat in the corner with the dumbbells lying around. Slowly he allows himself to feel happy. It
seems to him a beautiful letter, filled with the things the post-
cards lacked—well, maybe not filled with them, but unmis-
takably implying them. He has never been to Europe—never
traveled at all, except for his move to New York. (He does wonder, nervously, about their traveling together. How are these
things viewed in Europe? But Tim wouldn't have asked him
if it couldn't be made to work; people check into hotels all the
time, friends, rich men with Negro servants, maybe no one
thinks anything of it. Tim has traveled a lot; he'll know how
to do it.)

And the money for the plane ticket. He allows himself to
enjoy that too. And it has nothing to do with the money, he
tells himself, scrupulously (and not entirely accurately). It's the
feeling of being planned for, sent for.

There is nothing to be disappointed about.

He is fixing his lunch, laying slices of bologna on bread,
when it occurs to him that he'll have to ask for leave from
work, and that this might be difficult. Not because she would

refuse, but because it feels like the wrong time to go away. She is so unhappy now, beneath all the busy, vivid, energetic wit of the cat book. ("Guess what, Malcolm, I've figured out his family tree. He can trace his ancestry all the way back to . . . Catullus!" and then, the next night, "I've dropped the Catullus idea—I figured out something better.") And whenever she gets going, with sly, apparently detached amusement, on the subject of the Infant's cat, he wants to tell her to stop working so hard. He is glad to see her occupied, but it seems to him that there's a panicky, confected feeling to the project, that in fact it has the same quality she objected to, and was so hurt by, in that elaborate letter scheme of her husband's. It's as if, to guard against being humored in the future, she's decided to get in there first and humor herself.

Later, he walks to work in the snappy, deep blue late-winter afternoon, trying to figure out how he might bring up the subject of Europe. He's just gotten his key into the lock when the door is pulled open by Miss Soap Opera. Her face is somber and thrilled. "Something's happened."

"What?" he asks coolly. Her fervors automatically make him austere.

"I don't know what," she pants. "She made me put her back in the bed; she didn't want any lunch."

"Maybe she's sick. Did you call the doctor?"

"She wouldn't let me. Just wanted to be left alone, she said. I'm really worried. Would you like me to stay?"

"No, thanks, I'll be fine," he says, wondering as he has wondered before if this woman ever does or says anything that is not in character. He waits until she's actually out of the apartment—she is capable of lurking around, full of sympathy and meaning—before he goes and knocks gently at the bedroom door.

• • • •

"Malcolm?"

The bedside light is on, and there are books scattered on either side of her. She looks fine. "Are you okay?"

"Oh, you mean . . ." She rolls her eyes at the doorway. So does he. "Yeah."

"She drove me absolutely bananas today. I just wanted to scream. She's just this big, damp, hovering, clucking—I don't know what—giant chicken. Giant hen. I don't *want* to be under her wing—ugh, who could breathe under there?"

He smiles. "But did something happen?"

She shakes her head. He waits, but she doesn't say anything.

He asks what she'd like for dinner. "I was thinking I might make us an omelet."

"You go ahead. I'm really not hungry."

He should try to get her to eat, especially if she didn't have lunch. Then he thinks: Wait a minute, she's a grown woman; if she lived alone she wouldn't have anybody pestering her to eat. "Would you like your door open or closed?" he asks instead.

"Open," she tells him. She likes the feeling that he is nearby, likes hearing the clink of dishes in the kitchen.

She lies there, staring at the ceiling. She left her husband's letter in the den after reading it this morning, but she remembers parts of it—they keep jabbing her. It's a real letter, the first one he's actually mailed from this trip, postmarked from Segovia two days after the tour ended in Barcelona.

"Your news from New York is wonderful. Here is ours from Spain," it said. He passed her request to the Infant—"but now must call Infanta, because in Spain. She will be happy to lend cat for unhappy love affair."

She imagines him and the Infant walking the bleached

streets of Segovia, or sitting over a bottle of wine in a white-washed restaurant, laughing and spurring each other into wilder, frothier notions about the cat's passions. She knows how it feels to walk down a street late at night, stumbling into each other, giddy with laughter.

"Also has idea that maybe you will put in pictures of dancers dancing with cats—thinks would be very funny, and willing to pose."

It went on, exuberant, bubbling over with joy about her book, full of suggestions—with his syntax and his excitement, she couldn't tell which ideas were his and which the Infant's. She sees that he is radiant with relief that now there will be a place where the three of them can all exist together. She wishes she'd never dreamed up this book. Or thought it necessary to prove her own sophisticated magnanimity by inviting the Infant inside. She feels as if she's asked someone into her house who has tracked mud on all the floors and then broken every stick of furniture in the place. It's an accident, the guest didn't mean to do it, but there's the dirt and there are the splinters.

And there is her husband, mistaking her desperate good manners for a genuine wish that the guest might visit more often—or even move in.

And there is she herself, standing in the wreckage thinking that the only thing to do now is to put down white carpeting and set out some even more precious, fragile chairs.

"Just checking to see if you need anything," Malcolm says from the doorway.

"I'm fine," she says.

.   .   .

. . . .

Clearly she's not fine. He goes back into the kitchen and absently puts the other half of the omelet—the one he'd hoped she would say she was hungry for, when he looked in on her just now—into the refrigerator and carries his own plate into the living room.

He eats, reading *The New Yorker* but not remembering a word of it; he is just a pair of eyes moving down a page. He is imagining Europe, which he finds he can't do. Museums, buildings, languages, food—what is all that? It's an expanse, a vista he can feel the magnitude of without seeing clearly what it will be like; something inside him has gotten larger at the thought that he's going to go there. All he can actually picture, for some reason, are the Impressionist paintings he's seen in the Metropolitan of café scenes, the women in bustles and feathered hats, the whiskered men in evening clothes. Where would he be, in those paintings?

He thinks of Tim. The warm thing that he already feels like he's flying toward.

I wish he were smarter. I wish he loved me more.

Those things are true, but they don't matter. You don't want to go to someone because of a list—tall, red-gold hair, a kind of careless princely ease in the world—and there is no list that can stop you from wanting to go.

The apartment is very quiet.

The apartment is quiet. What is Malcolm doing out there? She wants him with her and she doesn't want anyone with her. She wants obliteration. She calls out, "Malcolm." When he comes, she asks him to bring her some brandy.

On an empty stomach? she hears him thinking. The other

aides (not de-carcass anymore, not now, anyway, she's so tired of her own peppy humor) would have said it, the Fräulein (no, her real name was Katie) with a quaver; and Betty, with dramatic relish.

Malcolm goes out and comes back with the drink.

He's poured it generously, not wanting to appear to be rationing her. "Would you like a drink too?" she asks. He hesitates for a moment. This has never come up before. He wants to be sharp, to be able to take care of her; but he doesn't want to seem prudish. And also: he'd like a drink.

"Bring it in here," she says. "Come sit for a while. And Malcolm?" she says, and he looks back at her questioningly.

"There's a letter on the desk. Can you go in and read it? And then come back, but please don't say anything about it."

When he returns after a few minutes with his own glass of brandy, she looks at his face and then looks away so she won't start crying.

After a while she asks for more, and he brings it. Why should she not get drunk if she wants to?

She asks him to turn out the light. They stay there together without talking. Finally he sees that she is asleep, and he goes to the living room and sits on the couch and falls asleep also. In his sleep he hears her calling his name over and over; and then he is awake and she is still calling him, screaming his name.

He runs into the bedroom, flipping on the overhead light so that the room is suddenly, starkly illuminated, the whole scene.

• • • •

She is sobbing, he has never seen her cry before. "It's all right, it's all right," he says, already pulling the covers off the bed, running to the bathroom to fill a basin with warm water and grab some washcloths. The sound of her crying pierces him like nothing ever has; his hands are shaking as he cleans her; his voice shakes as he tells her again and again that it's all right.

"I'm so ashamed," she manages to say at one point.

"It's not your fault, it was the brandy on an empty stomach, it could happen to anyone," he says, and she cries:

"No, I don't mean *this*," waving a hand to encompass the mess.

"All right, all right, all right," he continues to murmur.

He leaves her once he's cleaned her up, to run into the bathroom and set up the contraption so that he can rinse her. But when he wraps her in a clean sheet and carries her in there and she sees it, she starts to cry again. "No, please, no." She is shivering.

"All right," he says again. He carries her out of the bathroom and lays her gently on the floor of the hallway, with a folded towel under her head.

Lying there, she watches him leaning over the tub, detaching the hose from the tap and then lifting the contraption and folding it. The door half shuts while he replaces it on the hook where it lives, and then the door swings inward, opening again, so that she can see him going over to the tub and turning on the water. A bath—is he going to give her a bath? She hasn't had one for years. They tried it a few times, in the early days, her husband and an aide; but the tub is surrounded by tiled walls on three sides and there is no way for someone kneeling beside it to keep her neck and shoulders from sliding under without putting her in a stranglehold. After a few attempts that left her with bruises, the idea was abandoned; and as with all these failed experiments, she hasn't wasted time on regrets.

But hearing the hot water thundering into the tub, seeing the steam rise, she is suddenly filled with longing. She wonders how Malcolm will manage it, while knowing that he will. He's sitting on the edge of the tub, with his hand under the running water, as if testing the temperature, and his body twisted away from her. She can't see his face. After a while he stands up. She watches as he takes off his shirt and steps out of his trousers. He leaves on his briefs. She looks at his body, which is tall and very beautiful, as beautiful as the body of any dancer. He is neither looking at her nor looking away.

He is very calm, not worrying about any of this even though it is so far outside anything he has ever done. He knows it will be all right. When the tub is full he turns off the water and then goes to her and leans down to unwrap the sheet. He carries her to the tub and steps in. He lowers himself, still holding her crosswise, and then turns her so that she's lying on her back on top of him, her body resting along the length of his. He has his arm across her chest, supporting her; his hand is just beneath her right breast, which looks very white around the nipple's pink bloom. He has never looked at her body in this way—it's the thing he takes care of, and anyway, he wouldn't—but lying here beneath her, he feels himself getting hard. It doesn't matter, she can't feel it so it won't scare her; and it doesn't scare him. They rest together in the hot green water.

．　　　．　　　．

• • • •

There's the warmth of the water—acutely lovely where it envelops her upper body; but also, surprisingly, something she can feel in her legs, without having any other sensation there. There's the weightlessness. There is the warm, prickly, solid support of Malcolm's body against her upper back and shoulders. There's his brown arm lying across her whiteness, his hand near her breast: the assurance and gentleness of it. There's his chin resting lightly on the top of her head. There's the sight of their bodies in the shimmering water, her own nakedness stretched out so lightly along his. She has not felt like this in a long time; and some of it is new to her, tonight.

After a while she asks him if he'd like to hear a story.

"Yes," he says.

"This is one my husband tells. I think it's my favorite," she says; and it seems normal and relaxed, too, that she should speak of her husband.

Once, she begins, *there was a fisherman who lived by the River Volkov. There were many pretty girls in his town, but none so beautiful as his lovely little river. At night the fisherman sat on the bank and played his mandolin and sang love songs to the river.*

One night, when he'd had too much to drink, he fell asleep for a little while, and when he woke in the moonlight he saw a great blue-green head rising out of the river: the Tsar of the Waters. The tsar said, "My daughters and I have enjoyed your singing. Will you promise to come and visit us someday?"

"I promise," said the fisherman.

"I would like to give you a present," said the tsar. "When I am gone, cast your net into the river."

The tsar's head sank beneath the surface, and the fisherman threw in his net and felt it grow heavy. He pulled it out and there was a chest, and when he opened it he saw that the chest was full of jewels.

He sold some jewels and became rich, but still in the evenings he would sit on the bank and sing his love songs, and sometimes he would throw a bracelet or necklace into the river, because it was so beautiful.

Then he went traveling. He was on a ship, and suddenly, in the middle of the ocean, the ship stopped and would not move. "It's the Tsar of the Waters," the sailors said. "There must be someone on this ship he wants." So they all drew straws, and the fisherman got the short straw and remembered his promise. "That's right, the Tsar of the Waters does want me," he said, and he jumped over the side of the ship; and right away the ship began to move again.

The fisherman sank down, down, to the bottom of the ocean, until he came to the door of the tsar's palace. "What took you so long?" the tsar asked him. "I got tired of waiting, so finally I had to send for you."

They ate and drank, and then the tsar said, "I would like you to marry one of my daughters." And he brought his daughters before the fisherman, and each was lovelier than the one before; but still, the fisherman thought that none was as pretty as his little river. But then the youngest daughter came, and the fisherman cried out: "This girl is as beautiful as my River Volkov."

And the tsar said, "That's funny, her name is Volkov."

The fisherman saw that she was wearing a necklace and bracelet, and they were some of the jewels he had thrown into the river.

And so they were married, and they went to her room together and were very happy. Before they slept, she said, "Will you always sit beside me at night and sing to me?"

And he said, "I promise."

And they fell asleep. In the night, his foot touched the foot of his bride, and it was so cold he woke up. The moon was shining, and he saw that he was lying on the ground, and one of his bare feet had slipped into the cold River Volkov, and he knew that he was still poor.

When she finishes, they lie there quietly for a moment.

· · · ·

Then Malcolm lifts his leg so that his foot touches one of hers. She can't feel it, but she sees it. She smiles and turns in his arms and she kisses him, not lingeringly but not briefly either. His hand moves, and for a moment her breast is resting in his palm. Then she turns her head away from him and closes her eyes, and he puts his hand back where it was, and they lie without moving until the water starts to cool.

Getting out is not as elegant as getting in. He's afraid of her wet body slipping out of his wet hands, so he drains the tub and they both get very cold waiting for it to empty, and then he has to squirm out from beneath her without letting her heels and buttocks bang down on the hard porcelain. His soggy briefs sag ridiculously as he drips all over the bathroom floor getting towels, and he wraps her up and puts her back on the hallway floor while he dries himself and grabs some spare clothing he keeps on the top shelf of the linen closet (but no underwear—the need for dry underwear at work has never arisen before). By the time he has remade her bed and come back to collect her, she is shivering on the floor.

And even once she is back in bed again, with Malcolm sitting in the tweed armchair beside her, it takes a long time for her to get warm.

The News from Spain

Driving to the interview, the biographer got lost. His wife, in the passenger seat, squinted at the piece of paper on which he'd scribbled the directions the day before. "Turn left at the Mobil station. Did you do that already?"

"Liza," he said, "do you see any Mobil stations out here?"

They were driving through a neighborhood of enormous houses set behind enormous fences.

"I'm just trying to—"

"I know," he said. "I'm sorry."

It was February, but there was no snow on the ground. Maybe it didn't snow much here, out by the ocean. They wouldn't have known. They'd flown in the day before from L.A., which is where he—his name was Charlie—had lived all his life. Liza was from the Northeast, but inland: a small college town in Vermont.

They were on their way to see a woman named Alice Carlisle (at least that's what Charlie thought her name was; later

• • • • •

she would correct him), who had been married to the race-car driver Denis Carlisle in the early 1960s. There had been a group of four drivers—The Four, the press had called them—who were always lumped together, written about together. They'd trained together, partied together, raced together. They'd had looks, brains, nerve, and an almost unearthly casual glamour: it was hard to believe, looking at the photographs, that there had ever been any real people who looked like this, much less the coincidence of four of them together in the same sport at the same time. Charlie, who was working on a group biography, had already interviewed the two who were still alive. One lived not far from him, in Orange County; and the other, who'd been hit by a car about ten years ago and lost part of his leg—how weird, to survive all those race tracks intact and then get slammed returning a video to Blockbuster—was now in an assisted-living place near Las Vegas.

Charlie had found Alice thanks to something that at first seemed terrible: a magazine article by another writer about Giles McClintock, one of The Four. The article was called "The Countess and the Race-Car Driver." Liza had seen the title on the magazine cover at the supermarket, and looked inside to see who the race-car driver was. Charlie would not have needed to look; he was aware that Giles had had an affair with an earl's wife that had gone on for a year or two and ended shortly after the death of the earl in mysterious circumstances. He had asked Giles about it, dutifully but queasily, in the residents' lounge at the assisted-living place in Nevada; Giles had said, "Jesus Christ, I can't believe all you guys are still asking about that. For the millionth time: no fucking comment." Which had made Charlie drop the subject, and which should, he said to Liza after she brought the magazine home, have been a tip-off that another writer was working on The Four.

Charlie had skimmed the article saying, "Shit. Shit. Shit."

Liza had tried to be comforting—"He might not be working on a book, and even if he is, it'll be different from your book"—and kept him company while he drank almost an entire bottle of pinot noir.

She was twenty-four, eight years younger than Charlie. The difference in their ages was starting to seem smaller to her than it had at first, when she'd been a student in his intro-to-journalism course and she had liked him for taking himself—and her—seriously.

Charlie had ended up getting in touch with the other writer; he couldn't stand waiting, not knowing, while that other book might be ticking somewhere like a bomb. But the other book was not about The Four—it was about scandals. In the course of the conversation, the writer had given Charlie some leads he'd gathered while researching the countess story. Among them was Alice's phone number.

So here they were, in a white rental car that had Iowa plates, though they'd picked it up at the airport in Boston this morning after spending the night at a hotel near the runways. Liza had left the curtains open and lain on her side in the enormous bed late, awake (still on California time), while Charlie slept next to her. On her other side, nestled loosely in the curve of Liza's body, the baby had sat up, solemnly shredding Kleenex. "Another airplane," Liza had whispered to her, every time one took off or landed.

Liza glanced back now at the baby, asleep in her car seat, her head slumped on her shoulder. "She's going to be hungry when she wakes up."

"So then you'll feed her," Charlie said. Then, "Sorry, Liza, I just can't seem to find my way back to the main road—"

"I know." What she knew was that he hadn't really wanted

to bring her and the baby along on this interview. He was worrying that they would make him look unprofessional, encumbered. Liza hadn't planned on it either. In fact, she had imagined spending the day in Boston, silently, in the aquarium, pushing the stroller up the ramp that spiraled around the big central tank, showing the baby the penguins and the sea lion show. But when Charlie had mentioned to Alice on the phone yesterday that he was traveling with his wife and daughter, Alice had said to bring them along, she would give them all lunch. Liza, changing a diaper on the desk in their hotel room, heard his side of the phone call, his hearty "yes"; and then she'd seen the look of dismay, anger almost, that lingered on his face when he'd hung up the phone, because "yes" had been the only answer he'd been able to come up with.

Early that morning Alice had taken the dogs for a walk on the beach. This was part of her job, but Marjorie had come with her. Marjorie often delegated something to Alice and then did it along with her, partly because she never quite trusted anyone else to do a task, however minor, as competently as she would have done it herself, and partly because they liked each other. (Which didn't mean that there weren't things—quite a lot of things—that annoyed each of them about the other.)

They walked fast, the dogs running ahead and then coming back to circle them, while the cold winter sunrise went on over the ocean. They talked, about a party Marjorie and Arch had been to the night before, about wanting to lose weight, about a biography of Georgia O'Keeffe they had both been reading. Marjorie had almost finished it; Alice said, "Well, I'm still in her early thwarted lonely years, but it's hard for me to feel the anguish since I know how it all turns out."

"Yes, we do know that, don't we?" Marjorie said, laughing. "We do know how it all turns out." She often laughed too hard about some little shared observation, Alice had noticed, as if the sharing were a strange, rare thing that, once arrived at, had to be lingered over, a truce, before Marjorie wandered back into her own lonely, exacting, impatient span of territory.

"Would you be able to stop by the library today?" Marjorie asked. "They called yesterday to tell me my books are in, the Edith Wharton I ordered from the main branch, and the new Anne Tyler."

"Oh, Edith Wharton, I love Edith Wharton," Alice said. (She had noticed that she tended to gush whenever she was preparing to disappoint or cross Marjorie.) "But actually, today might not be the best day for that. Unless they're open late?"

Marjorie was annoyed, as Alice had known she would be. She liked to request things in a voice of extreme graciousness, and if she found she couldn't get what she wanted (which did not happen very often), part of her annoyance came from having her graciousness exposed as a mere mannerism.

"*Thursday* is the late night," she told Alice. "You know they close at three all winter. It really is a little inconvenient for me not to have those books today, and I'm not planning to be anywhere near the library or I'd pick them up myself. Are you sure you couldn't manage to find the time?"

Here was where Alice's job was confusing. She was given a studio apartment and a salary—not as big as it would have been without the apartment, but generous nonetheless—and in exchange she walked the dogs, took the cars to be washed, and when Marjorie and Arch were away (they traveled a lot), collected mail, watered plants, and let piano tuners and upholsterers into and out of the house. Alice was supposed to jump

• • • • •

when Marjorie said "jump"—but it was confusing because they were sort of friends, and because Marjorie didn't think she ever said "jump."

On the whole, though, Alice felt she owed them a lot more than they owed her. Certainly they needed someone like her, a trustworthy errand runner and occasional caretaker. But they could manage without her—they would simply find someone else. Whereas she, without them, would be broke and alone.

She had met them eight years earlier, one night at a country club. They belonged to it; Alice was there as the guest of an old friend, a widow, whose husband had once directed Alice in a play in London. It was close to Christmas, and the club had been particularly festive—there had been an oyster bar, and a martini fountain, and an air, Alice thought, of tired, concocted opulence, as if the club had done this sort of thing so many times that it was sick of itself, going through the motions. Still, she enjoyed the whole thing—oysters, candlelight, the smell of balsam, men in black tie. She'd been flirting lightly with a quite attractive man when she'd noticed a tall woman in a dark red tunic with a million pleats coming toward them. Oh, Alice had thought, the wife. But then the three of them had ended up having a giddy, nutty conversation—afterward she couldn't remember the content (probably there hadn't been much), just the champagne-like fizz of it. They'd asked Alice and her friend to join them at dinner. Then they had invited Alice to the next few parties they'd thrown—they lived in one of the greatest of the great houses along the water—and then Alice and Marjorie had lunch together a few times.

Alice had been working as a bank teller then, which she'd started when she got out of real estate (before that she'd been a decorator, and before that an actress). She was coming up to the age for mandatory retirement, and trying not to think too much about what would come next. Something would turn up, she had to believe. What had turned up was that Marjorie, who drank at these lunches, said emphatically that this was perfect, Alice must come to her and Arch; they needed someone to look after them. A grown-up, said Marjorie, someone with imagination and a life of her own, not some stupid kid who would need to be told all the time what to do. Alice, who didn't drink at all anymore but got a lot of vicarious, nostalgic pleasure from watching other people do it, was touched by Marjorie, who had up until now merely amused her. "I will come," she had said, "and I will tell you right now, though I bet you won't want to hear it, that your grace and tact are just extraordinary."

So Alice had this perplexing, nuanced job, which had saved her life and which made saying even a rare "No" to Marjorie somewhat complicated and difficult. Alice thought it was a bit like a pinball machine, the "No" a little silver ball that you shot off as strategically as you could, but always with a sense of randomness, and then you stood and watched it ricocheting and bouncing off a series of moods and obligations and generous acts and small stored resentments and moments of gratitude and ingratitude, wondering curiously where it would come out. It might help to send another silver ball after it, to careen around and run into it, perhaps altering its course: an explanation.

"It's just that I have these young people coming to spend the day," she told Marjorie. "A writer, in fact. He's working on something about Denis."

"Oh, how exciting," Marjorie said, vexation apparently forgotten. "Now, is this the same one who was here—let's see, was it two years ago? Three?"

• • • • •

"No, that was a screenwriter," Alice said.

"And did anything ever happen about that? Do you hear from him?"

"He sent me a couple of Christmas cards, but not this past year. No, I'm sure I would have heard if a movie had actually been made."

"Yes, we'd probably notice that, wouldn't we?" Marjorie said, laughing. "We'd notice if we were at the movies and it was the story of Alice. I think we'd *notice*."

As they came up from the beach, with the inexhaustible dogs streaking ahead of them down the length of the pergola, webbed with winter-bare rose canes, Alice told Marjorie that she always felt a little peculiar when these writers showed up, because the truth was she didn't really remember all that much. "I don't mean that my memory's going. It's not about going gaga."

Marjorie frowned; this was not the kind of thing you said to her. Too personal, too confessional. Alice would have liked her just to nod, but Marjorie said briskly, "Well, I'm sure it will be fine. You remember plenty, I'm sure. And certainly, you're doing him a favor just to spend the time with him. He should be grateful for that. I certainly hope he *thanks* you. I certainly hope he knows to be *grateful*."

By the time they reached the kitchen door, Marjorie had grown even more indignant about the writer's anticipated ingratitude. It was her way, Alice thought, of offering solidarity: she didn't quite understand what she had been asked to give, but she knew she'd been asked to give something, and this at least felt like impassioned reciprocation. Marjorie interrupted herself, bending with a towel to dry one dog and tossing a towel for Alice to use on the other one, to ask if Alice needed anything to round out lunch. "I have some crab cakes in the freezer, I think; and there's a lot of that chicken left from the party the other night . . . No? Some soup?"

Alice said thanks, it was very nice of Marjorie (it was), but she was all set.

Charlie and Liza were almost an hour late, and were cowed by the sight of the house. "Oh, my God," Charlie said.

"It's like Gatsby," Liza said.

"I don't even know where to pull up. Which door, do you think?"

Alice, though, seemed to have been watching for them; she flew out to the car and was saying, "Welcome! Welcome!" before they'd even had a chance to climb out, looking somewhat dazedly around them. She had tousled hair, cut quite short, which was either dyed blond or else had turned the kind of white that is closer to yellow. Very blue narrow eyes, behind gold-rimmed glasses. A soft, drooping, nearly unwrinkled face. Red sweater, loose jeans. Her voice was a little hoarse. She had a wonderful smile.

"And who is this?" she was saying, bending to look into the backseat while Liza unclipped the straps of the car seat.

"This is Veronica," Liza said.

"Veronica!" Alice said to the baby, as Liza drew her out of the car. She'd woken up about fifteen minutes ago and, surprisingly, had not yet cried to be fed. "Your name is Veronica? Such a big name for such a little person." Alice was holding out her arms, glancing at Liza: "Will she let me?"

"Let's see," Liza said, handing over the baby.

"Veronica," Alice said softly, looking into the baby's face. "I think you may be the first Veronica I've ever met. What do you

• • • • •

think? Have you encountered many other Veronicas?" Veronica looked back at Alice with her usual mild gravity. Alice
laughed. "Ah. She's considering the question."

Still carrying Veronica, she led Liza and Charlie to a door
at the far end of the house where it angled and joined with a
row of large, old-fashioned garage doors, and then up a narrow
stairway to another door. "Here we are!"

It was a big, cream-colored room, with a row of windows at
the back. A worn couch and chairs on a balding Persian rug.
A couple of low white bookcases. A galley kitchen against one
wall; a single bed, covered with a tan comforter, on the other.

Liza went to the windows and saw hedges wrapped in bur-
lap, long beds covered with hay, brown-yellow grass, more garden beyond, big cold gray sky, and, from the last window, a
small slice of dark gray ocean. Charlie saw that he was going
to have to find a tactful way to ask Alice about her position in
this household; clearly she was not, as he had imagined when
they first drove up, the wife of a billionaire. Although: Was her
current situation really relevant to his project? Was he going
to introduce himself, and today, into the book? *I finally found
Alice in a one-room garage apartment attached to a fabulously grand
house?* Or was he just going to write straight history—*In 1958
(or whenever it was) Denis Carlisle met a young woman named
Alice at* (wherever they had met)—objectively planting Alice in
the part of her past that mattered to the book and leaving her
there?

Alice made coffee, and Charlie pulled out his notebook (he
hated to use a tape recorder: not the process of using it but the
dullness of the transcript afterward. He felt that sending tapes
out to be transcribed was like sending a suit out to be cleaned
and having it run over by a steam roller instead—it came back
so flattened that it was unrecognizable. For him, reading tran-

scripts of his own interviews was the opposite of verification; a transcript made him doubt what he knew he'd heard).

They sat on the couch and began with the basics: Where were you born? What did your parents do? How many brothers and sisters? Alice answered with an air of eager cooperation that Charlie hadn't seen in any of the other people he'd interviewed. Some had been grumpy and impatient (Giles), some straightforwardly factual, or wistful, or thoughtful and almost dreamy, finding that the interview process took them back to things they hadn't thought about in years. But he'd never seen anybody lay herself bare as—as *cheerfully,* he would later say to Liza.

(But that would come later, in the car, driving to Vermont, that debriefing with Liza. Checking in with her—*You were there, what did you think?*—which would feel satisfying to Charlie in some ways, and not in others. *You were right there, Liza—why are you acting as though you weren't?*)

Right now, jotting down preliminary facts about Alice, he was faintly annoyed that Liza was there, and a little embarrassed at being his professional (serious, earnest, slightly full of shit) self in front of her. She sat nursing Veronica in one of the chairs, her knees practically touching the arm of the couch where he and Alice sat. He was listening to Alice, nodding, writing things down—but he kept seeing Liza there, without actually quite looking at her, and he kept thinking, Could you at least go over and sit on the bed? (But Alice had, quite deliberately, placed her in the chair, saying it was the most comfortable place to sit.)

Liza knew how he was feeling, and was trying not to let it faze her. If there had been another room to go into, she would have gone into it, but there wasn't. She was feeling peaceful—relatively peaceful, anyway—sitting there in the

· · · · ·

sun, with the baby's hand gently kneading the skin just above her breast. Veronica, fresh from her nap, drank but looked around curiously, aware of being in a new place. She had fine dark curls that weren't even quite curls yet, more like half curls; they always seemed optimistic to Liza, and, combined with Veronica's grave demeanor, they could make her want to cry.

Alice was saying that her parents had not approved of her going to New York at the age of nineteen to become an actress, but they had kissed her and given her money and put her on the train, "with all the love in the world," she said. "They didn't understand, so they couldn't quite give me their blessing; but they trusted me and wanted me to be happy, and I was."

She'd gotten married a few months later, she said, to a very young actor. "Because we wanted so much to go to bed together. We'd both been taught, you see, that one didn't have sex outside marriage, and we both believed it. And what's really funny is that we both believed everyone else believed it too." She laughed. "So: the belief didn't last long, and neither did the marriage."

Then she'd had a few years of being what she called "a sort of hot young actress."

She got up and pulled an album from the bookshelf and sat with it open on her lap. There she was in an eighteenth-century French farce, with a laced bodice and a curly white wig; there in some modern drama smoldering in a dark cocktail dress and smoking; there looking plaintive ("Sonya in *Uncle Vanya*," she said); there in some sort of showgirl costume, with fishnet stockings and a bunch of bananas on her head.

Liza put Veronica, who had finished eating, down on the floor and leaned over to look at the pictures. She saw that Alice had been very beautiful: a kind of frank, at-ease, lush beauty that was at once erotic and friendly. Even as Sonya, where they must have tried to deglamorize her, she shone. Liza reached her hand toward the Chekhov photo, and Alice said, "Well, that was a mistake. Not for me to do it—it was fascinating—but for them to cast me. I was the hot name for a little while, so they were casting me in everything, and I was lucky to get all that attention. But the truth was, I just wasn't that good an actress."

Charlie was writing some things down, Liza saw, but not as much as she would have liked him to. He was humoring Alice a little bit—maybe not quite humoring her, nothing quite so condescending, but he was letting her talk about things he didn't need to know about so that she'd be relaxed by the time they got to the important stuff. Liza was disappointed in him, and a bit miffed on Alice's behalf: this *was* good stuff.

But Alice seemed to notice at the same time how few notes Charlie was taking, and she laughed. "Oh, my God, here I am going on and on, and we haven't even started talking about Denis. Fire away."

Denis. Liza saw Charlie jump a little, hearing the name—the name in the books, in the newspaper clippings, in the obsessive history-of-car-racing websites, the name on the timeline chart of The Four that Charlie had inked out on poster board on the living room floor a couple of years ago and which had hung on the wall over his desk ever since, the name that Charlie pronounced so seriously as a history name, a biography name—tossed carelessly into the conversation. She knew why the name, spoken casually by Alice who had been his wife, had this kind of effect on Charlie. Denis Carlisle had been killed at the age of twenty-six, in a race outside Barcelona. His car had skidded off the road and flipped into a tree, and his helmet had shattered.

• • • • •

It was the kind of death that both was and was not supposed to happen—shocking, tragic, pointless—but wasn't that part of what racing was for? Or any dangerous sport. Death was always the thing that could happen; it needed to happen sometimes, or the risk would not be real.

Yes: Denis, Liza wanted to say to Charlie. *Not some mythic figure. Her husband. Just listen.*

Alice had gotten up again, and was kneeling on the bed, taking down some framed black-and-white photographs from a group that hung on the wall. She came back and handed them to Charlie. One was a close-up of a man's face: tanned, handsome, squinting into the sun, windblown light hair, intelligence, humor, grace—a set of blessings that couldn't help but seem doomed; it was impossible to look and not romanticize him, even for Liza, who badly wanted not to, she just wanted to let him be a regular guy caught on film in an ordinary moment.

The other two photographs went together. A group of men around a table in a nightclub. Sitting on the knee of the most beautiful of the men was a woman in a dress that was tight in the bodice and then extravagant in the skirt, billowing over the man's legs and trailing onto the floor. The other people at the table were smiling, but the man and woman were roaring, their heads thrown back, their eyes closed and mouths wide open, their beautiful throats exposed. The next photograph had been taken a moment later: they'd stopped laughing and were leaning toward each other, looking at each other. The look right before you kiss the one person whose existence strikes you as both necessary and miraculous.

Liza, who knew something of this feeling, who had struggled with it for years (sometimes it was better, sometimes almost unbearable—this was something separate, it had nothing to do with Charlie or with her marriage, though she knew she had married Charlie partly as an attempt to solve the problem), took the photograph from Charlie and looked at it for a while.

"That was at El Morocco," Alice said, "the winter we got married."

"I have to ask this," Charlie said, "even though I know it's an incredibly dumb question, but: Do you remember what was so funny?"

The biographer was fine, Alice thought. A mail-order biographer. *Send me one biographer,* you wrote on the form, and this was what you'd get. A perfectly nice, serious, competent young man.

But the wife was more interesting. So young! (But maybe not that young—older than she'd been when she'd married Fred, and Denis, too, for that matter. It was just that they looked younger nowadays. *We looked so old, with the hair and the clothes and the heels and the makeup. But that's what we wanted, to look old. Sophisticated. The desirable word, the high compliment.*) She admired Liza's long, straight black hair, her calm face. It was unusual, Alice thought, this combination of self-containment and warmth. Liza didn't say much: How was it, then, that Alice felt so certain of her goodwill?

They were taking a break from the interview; the two of them were getting the lunch, while Charlie fleshed out his notes and kept an eye on Veronica, who sat on the floor playing with some empty Tupperware containers Alice had put down in front of her.

"I hoped I was pregnant," Alice said, "right after Denis died, but it was probably good that I wasn't."

Liza, at the stove stirring the soup, looked at her.

"Well, because I wasn't really a responsible person for a number of years after that. A lot of years. I was drinking quite a bit. And flying here and there for acting jobs, trying to have a career. And living in one city, then another." Alice smiled. "I was a mess."

It was strange, she thought, getting down a platter for the cold meats and cheeses, that she could narrate all this, her life, and not feel any of it.

Her AA sponsor was fond of saying, "My life is an open book." Alice, who liked the candor of AA (not all the hokey slogans, though), wondered if that was it. Standing up in front of meetings, talking to various friends over decades, telling things to writers (one showed up to interview her every couple of years, although most of the projects never seemed to get finished): the more you talked about your life, the less real it seemed. Maybe she'd told her story so many times that it had become just that: a story. What do I know about my life that no one else knows? she thought.

If she closed her eyes and tried to conjure up Denis's face, what she saw was the photographs. The man squinting in the sun, the man sitting in the car, the man laughing back at her from the deck of the boat they'd lived on in Monte Carlo harbor. What had his bare back looked like, his thighs, the palms of his hands? What had his face looked like in bed, what things had he said to her, how had his voice sounded when he said them?

It wasn't that she didn't have the information, the adjectives she needed to answer her own questions, up to a point. *Strong. Warm. Tender. Helpless and elated.* It was that the words were all she knew. The words both preserved and eradicated the past; at some point they had replaced it.

Liza held the baby in her lap during lunch, feeding her soup with an old demitasse spoon that Alice had run down to borrow from Marjorie's silver chest. Charlie kept asking questions and taking notes, not eating much. Alice was liking him better—he certainly knew a lot about Denis. More, in fact, about Denis's career than she knew herself.

"Oh, yes," he said, "that was Bavaria, 1961."

"Was it?" Alice said.

They had covered everything. Now the three of them were waiting, sitting at the table with the afternoon sun making a drama of the dirty lunch dishes, to talk about Denis's death.

"I know this must be a painful subject," Charlie began.

"No, it's all right," Alice said gently. She felt sorry for him. "Remember, it's over forty years ago."

"You weren't with him there, were you?"

She shook her head. "I'd gone to Paris, to visit friends."

"And so—well, I guess I'm wondering how you felt, when you got the news from Spain."

The news from Spain. Oh, dear God, "the news from Spain"! Spoken in that deep ponderous undertaker voice. The unctuous importance of it, as if he were saying: The news from Hiroshima. The news from Dallas. *Lighten up, Charlie,* she felt like telling him.

Her eyes met Liza's, and she saw that they were united, somehow, against Charlie's solemn ardor. But she also felt an obligation to protect his dignity.

She made her own voice serious and hushed. "Well, it was terrible," she said. And it had been. But at the moment she was feeling pretty jaunty. In fact, she was afraid that if her eyes met Liza's again, she might start laughing.

She went on, though, in the serious voice: She had been

staying with Michael and Sylvia Webster, an American couple she and Denis had met at a party in Cannes and become quite close to. She and Sylvia had been out shopping, and when they came home at teatime Michael, unusually, was there. He was with the diplomatic service; they had a teletype machine in the office. He had already arranged for Alice to fly to Barcelona, though there was no hurry by that point. It always seems like you have to hurry, even when it's too late. It's also so strange, Alice said, what you remember from a time like that. No memory whatsoever of the flight, or anything about Barcelona. What I remember was the shaving kit—Sylvia had taken me that day to a beautiful leather-goods store on the rue Saint-Honoré, and I'd bought Denis a shaving kit; and that's the thing I really remember about the days right after his death: how the thought of that shaving kit could just undo me. They asked me if I wanted to see Denis, she added, and I knew that I definitely did not.

Charlie was scribbling and looking stricken, she saw. Liza's face, too, was creased and sad.

All this was new to them. It was a terrible story.

"An adventure! Are you ready for an adventure?" Alice said to Veronica, when Liza had put her in the baby carrier and strapped it onto her chest, so that Veronica faced forward. She hung in the harness tilted out and slightly downward, like the figurehead of a ship.

They were walking down to the beach with the dogs; they had left Charlie on Alice's couch with a box of letters and photographs. "Fair game," Alice had told him. "Anything you want, really. We can go into town later and make photocopies."

The dogs were running around like crazy. The baby laughed and screamed at them, pointing, kicking her legs. "They're pretty silly, aren't they?" Alice said. She unlatched a gate and they walked along a short boardwalk and then down some steps onto the beach. The strong, cold wind exhilarated Liza, and she laughed. She and Alice both started to run. The ocean was the color of slate, enormous. The waves ran very fast, halfway between the shoreline and the horizon, forming white tops that skidded toward each other and joined. They were the same each time, but they seemed, somehow, impulsive, a series of sudden whims.

After a few minutes Liza and Alice slowed to a walk, breathing hard but, as Alice pointed out, warmer. The baby's cheeks were flaming; she watched, yearning but not making any sound, as the dogs went on running, away from them.

"So," Alice said to Liza, "and what do you do?"

"Oh." The question startled Liza, maybe because she'd spent so much of the day as an observer. "Well, I'm a musician."

"Really? What kind of music?"

"Early music."

"How early?" Alice, still panting from the run, sounded eager, and was looking at Liza with real interest.

So Liza talked, about the consort tradition and how it had led into the baroque, which Alice turned out to know something about because she had a friend in London who was a choral conductor. "Purcell," she said. "He'd be an example of one of those transitional guys, right?"

"Exactly," Liza said. "What I play are the stringed instruments—lute, dulcimer—"

"Theorbo," Alice said, surprisingly.

Liza laughed. "Theorbo."

. . . . .

"Impressive, aren't I? But let me tell you something: I know that there is such a thing, but I have absolutely no idea what it is."

"It's like a two-headed lute."

"And *hautbois d'amour*. That was the other terrific name I remember. 'High wood of love.' But again: could not tell you the first thing about it if my life depended on it."

Liza, looking into Alice's red-cheeked, animated face, felt suddenly lacerated, such an unexpected rawness that she forgot to breathe. "Well, it's an oboe," she said finally. "*Hautbois:* oboe. You can see where the word comes from—"

"An oboe," Alice said. "How interesting." Then, "How . . . disappointing. It sounds like it should be something more than an oboe. Something more *courtly*."

"The oboe d'amour is tuned a third lower than a regular oboe," Liza went on automatically. "But otherwise it's pretty similar. My cousin David plays both."

They walked a few more steps, then Liza said, "I'm in love with him." She felt relieved an instant before she said it—before she even quite knew she would say it.

Alice stopped and turned to face her. They stood looking at each other for a moment. Then Alice said, "Oh, my dear," and put her arms around Liza and held her—loosely, because the baby was between them, but for a long time.

Alice was not the first person Liza had told this to. She had talked to a psychologist when she first came to California halfway through her sophomore year of college. That was right after David, who was two years older, had, suddenly and without telling Liza of his plans, gotten married. Their affair had all taken place in the summers, when his family came and opened their house outside the town where Liza's family lived in Vermont. Liza had fallen in love with him at thirteen and slept with him since the summer when she was fifteen. She was shattered. She had driven to his college to talk to him; he'd permitted her to question him, horribly, in the vestibule of his apartment building, because his wife was upstairs. Liza, knowing that she was desperate and that the questions were useless, tried anyway to ask him about his marriage—Why hadn't he at least let her know in advance?—but he, white-faced, had not only refused to talk about it but acted as if he didn't understand why she was so upset. It was as if he had amnesia, Liza had said later to the shrink in California, or as if he was implying that I'd made the whole thing up.

The shrink had talked to her about incest, how it was always a complicated violation of some sort. "But I wanted to!" Liza had said. "Even then," the doctor gently insisted.

And the other person Liza had talked to, her friend Amanda (who'd been her roommate at UCLA), had called David "that prick" or "that exploitative asshole cousin of yours"—which gratified the part of Liza that was angry and hurt, but left the part of her that still loved David feeling lonely and wrong.

No one had ever known—Liza herself had not known—that what she wanted was for someone to hold her and say, "Oh, my dear."

She bathed in it, was infinitely soothed; and yet, in some way she couldn't understand, she was also saddened.

(Years later, when Liza was divorced from Charlie and long since over David, and she thought of this conversation, she would still wonder about that sadness. Some of it had been for herself, certainly. But some, she had come to feel—and hoped she'd felt back then—had had to do with Alice. Wanting to say "Oh, my dear" back to Alice, and feeling too young and shy to say it.)

．　．　．　．　．

．　　．　　．

It was when they got back from the beach that Charlie asked Alice about her name. "I thought it was Alice Carlisle, but all these letters are addressed to Alice Montgomery."

"Yes, that was my maiden name, and my stage name. I went back to it after Denis died. And I never even bothered taking my third husband's name, which turned out to be smart, because that was another short marriage." In fact, it had lasted just over a year: the English choral conductor she'd mentioned to Liza on the beach.

"I'm glad we straightened that out," Charlie said. "That would have been pretty bad, to get your name wrong."

"Well, but not the end of the world," Alice said.

They were getting ready to leave, gathering the baby's things, which had somehow spread themselves over the room: a rattle on the floor, a box of wipes and a changing pad on the kitchen counter, a cloth book about animals sticking up between the cushions of the couch. Charlie was fretting because he'd made a pile of things to take to be photocopied, but they were running late; they needed to drive to Vermont tonight; Liza's family was expecting them.

On the beach, Alice had heard about the Vermont plan: it was going to be a weekend-long family reunion, and it would be the first time Liza had seen David since that night in the vestibule of his apartment building. "So I have a baby, and he has three-year-old twins," she had told Alice. "We'll both be well insulated. But I'm scared."

"That you'll feel it, or that you won't feel it?"

"Both. It would be terrible either way. But I think I'll feel it."

"I think so too," Alice had said. She had asked Liza about her marriage to Charlie, and Liza had said she thought it was good.

"I really do. We do love each other. And Veronica—we're both crazy about her, and Charlie's a great father. But also: it's me trying to play by the book."

"Which can almost work sometimes," Alice had said.

Now, gently, she told Charlie not to worry: she would photocopy the stuff he wanted over the next day or so, and mail it to him.

"Are you sure?" he asked, and she wanted to hug him too, as she had Liza.

She walked them out to their car and watched them stow Veronica in the car seat, and then she did hug them both, and they thanked her for everything and she said, "Oh, please." Then they said they would stay in touch and she waved them off, imagining the Christmas cards.

It was getting dark, the sudden darkness that falls over the Atlantic in winter: a somber shutting down, the ocean withdrawing and becoming invisible. She went back upstairs and ran herself a bath. Undressing near the bathroom window, she saw a low shape running lightly through the garden: a fox.

She lay in the hot water wishing for gin. Not that she'd ever actually take the drink, after all these years—you make the phone call, you go to a meeting, the whole boring yet weirdly effective catechism—but just remembering that old feeling of the first few sips, that first inkling that you were going to begin to relax and feel warm. It would be pleasant, that was all she was thinking.

Her body rippled under the water, loose and white. Good-bye, Marilyn and Sophia (God, those photographs from earlier!). Hello, Pillsbury Doughboy.

But it was okay. This was what people looked like at her age. Denis, if he were here, would be old too.

• • • • •

She got out of the bath and dried herself and got dressed, in a pair of black silk pants and a beige cashmere tunic that had once belonged to Marjorie. Marjorie had invited her for dinner tonight, and she found she was looking forward to it, although she also knew she would have been just fine alone.

She walked through the house and found Arch by himself in the library off the entry hall. Marjorie was home, he said, but not down yet. "What can I get you, Alice? Gibson? Sidecar? Sazerac sling?"

"Ha, ha," Alice said gamely. She assumed this gameness automatically, having learned over the years that it was the only way to deal with Arch. "A little cranberry juice and soda, thanks."

He handed it to her and went back to his wing chair. "So Marge tells me you've had the press in today. You granted them an audience, your public? The paparazzi too?"

"No, just a very nice young writer and his wife. He's working on a biography of Denis and the others."

"And we can expect a movie?" Arch went on. "We should be holding our breath for a major motion picture?"

"Well, Arch, one of these days you just might be surprised," Alice said, still in that plucky chirp she used with him.

In fact, Charlie had told her he was working on a movie treatment as well as his book, and was planning to show it around to people in Hollywood.

Alice, watching Arch sip his whiskey and soda, thought suddenly that if there ever was a movie, there'd be a scene set in El Morocco, and an actress would sit on an actor's knee and laugh and then he'd kiss her. There would be a lot of takes; at the end of the day the actress would go home thinking how tired she was of laughing and being kissed.

Arch seemed suddenly aware that she was watching his glass. His eyes narrowed. "So, how's your higher power today, Alice?"

"Just fine, Arch," she said evenly.

So: after all there were things about her life that she'd never told anyone. Here, right now, were two things she knew that no one else did. The way Arch talked to her, and the fact that, like almost everything else, it never seemed to get to her.

The News from Spain

Voi che sapete che cosa è amor . . .
(You who know what love is . . .)

CHERUBINO TO ROSINA,
Le Nozze di Figaro, MOZART AND DA PONTE

Voi sapete quel che fa.
(You know what he always does.)

LEPORELLO TO ELVIRA,
Don Giovanni, MOZART AND DA PONTE

I

Years later, long after what most people thought of as the real action was over, Rosina and Elvira met and became friends. They had exiled themselves from their old lives. Rosina was divorced, and Elvira hadn't seen Johnny in years. They met in a cooking class, which both had signed up for distractedly, thinking it might be good for them.

One week it was raining on the night the class met. The windows steamed up, the room smelled delicious, and no one could tell what was happening outside. Rain slapped blindly on the glass. By the time they all loaded the dishwashers, wiped the counters, and went outside just after ten, the storm had strengthened. Rosina and Elvira stepped out of the building together. The wind was blowing the rain in stinging sideways gusts, and the dark trees in the square were tossing their limbs and creaking.

"Come home with me," Rosina said.

Elvira was startled. Over the weeks they had smiled at each other, chopped together, talked a little bit in the ladies' room. It was one of those incipient friendships that might or might not develop: the thing that made it possible—a recognition of and respect for the other's reserve—was the same thing that would probably prevent it from happening.

"I'll be all right," Elvira told Rosina as they stood on the doorstep. Driving out to the country, she meant. She said it automatically, but looking at the wildly rocking trees, she wasn't sure it was true. She was surprised and touched that Rosina had remembered, from some polite little conversation weeks ago, that she didn't live in town.

"Come on," Rosina said, already beginning to run.

Even the drive across the city was frightening—sheets of rain on the windshield; floods in the streets; the old plane trees along the river shuddering and luminous, with paler patches where branches were shearing off; the river rocking and spitting in its banks. "You were right," Elvira said at the end of it. "I couldn't have driven home in this."

Rosina lived in a tall old row house, the kind that had generally long since been divided into apartments. But this one

．　．　．　．　．　．

hadn't been. It was calmly intact, and of a scale that made Elvira suddenly shy. There were plain, pale modern sofas, and dark carved chests, and old rugs; there were paintings that Elvira would have liked to stop and gape at; there was a Vuillard oil in the library, where a fire was already laid, waiting for Rosina to touch it with a match.

They sat there, having showered, wearing Rosina's nightgowns and robes, drinking cognac, with a plate of oranges and chocolate. *What is all this?* Elvira wanted to ask. She was dazzled, and a little disappointed in herself for being dazzled. She was habitually austere. She lived simply, because she chose to—her income as a painter was erratic, and she wanted to keep as much time as possible free for painting. She'd been around money before, had rich friends, hung around with rich people who bought her paintings. But this, Rosina's house, wasn't just money—it was something else, something unfathomable.

Rosina was asking her about her work—what kind of painting did she do?—and Elvira was giving tight little answers, as if she were on a job interview.

"I'm sorry," Rosina said. "I'm prying. I know a lot of artists don't like talking about their work."

"No, no, it's fine," Elvira said. Then they were both silent. She felt she was letting Rosina down, being a dull, graceless guest.

Finally Elvira asked about the pictures in the house—she was dying to, they were screaming at her, and it seemed pretentiously nonchalant to ignore them. They walked around and looked at everything, barefoot, carrying their drinks. Elvira, who hated it when people talked in museums, didn't say anything, just smiled at Rosina from time to time, and once laughed out loud, standing in front of a Goya that was hanging in the dining room, a toothy, inane-faced portrait of a woman with many jewels in her hair. Rosina laughed too. "You always wonder how he got away with it," she said.

When they sat down again in front of the fire, it was different. They were peaceful, the awkwardness was gone. The late hour, the storm still slashing away outside and beating on the old window glass, the pictures, the brandy, the deep quiet of the house.

In a book they would have told each other their stories then. They would have been stranded together for a night, high above their ordinary lives: travelers at an inn, fleeing a city in which there was plague; or refugees from a shipwreck crowded into a lifeboat; or survivors of a war holed up in a villa. The threat of death would have hovered, recently and narrowly escaped, possibly still imminent. They would have told their stories without fear, with a reckless noble end-of-the-world candor.

But there was no plague, no shipwreck. The storm was dramatic but not deadly; it was just a late-winter rainstorm. Elvira and Rosina were both guarded, discreet, even secretive people; that wasn't going to change. They told each other a little bit that night; they made forays. Rosina talked about her grown son—she had moved to this city to be near him and his wife and their two small daughters; Elvira was here because she'd lucked into a small house in the country, with a barn she could use as a studio. But something bigger happened too, an alliance, an unspoken agreement that this would be a patient and safe friendship. They would come to know each other slowly, over time.

• • • • • •

2

It would have been nice, impressive, to write: *The countess left Aguas Frescas, taking nothing.* But on second thought, why? Who over the age of twenty would be impressed by such shortsighted renunciation? The lawyers had worked out a decent settlement. And Rosina had wanted a number of things. A few of the smaller paintings, her pearls (though none of the other jewelry), money. She sent word to her husband through the housekeeper that she would like to take some furniture from obscure corners of the house, nothing much, nothing that would leave any room looking plundered. Not even anything from her bedroom—those sad pieces of furniture, paced between, stared at, cried on, collapsed on: they were part of what she was leaving.

Her husband sent word back that she should take whatever she wanted. He was being fair, reasonable, as he almost always was, except when he wanted something that fairness and reason couldn't easily obtain. Even then, he could cloak his unreasonableness by pointing out hers. "Look what you're doing to yourself," he would say, when she had wept and stormed at him after learning of some new infidelity.

I can stand this, she had thought at first. Well, not at first. At first there had been nothing to stand. They were happy. They ran the estate, which included a large and very successful vineyard; they went riding and fishing together; they spent time in the city and went to parties and concerts, bought clothes and books; they were ecstatic and abandoned in bed together. "No," she would murmur, "no, don't," and that was part of the game, for him to overcome her.

For the first few years they would travel abroad together

in connection with the wine business. Then he started saying that one of them should stay home and oversee, as he put
it, "domestic operations." These trips were boring, anyway,
he said. You stay here, and we'll go someplace in the spring.
Paris, or New York. So he stopped taking her with him. From
the rumors she began hearing of his travels, she surmised a
wife would have been an encumbrance. *She surmised.* Listen to
the coolness of that, the hard-won worldliness. When she first
learned of his infidelities, she was shattered. But eventually she
came to feel that as long as his dalliances were conducted while
he was away, they had nothing to do with her. She even felt a
dim sense of gratitude at his discretion, seeing it as a mark of
his respect and tenderness for her (and seeing at the same time
the self-abasement inherent in such gratitude).

I can stand this, she thought.

But then he fell for someone at home, one of the maids. Her
personal maid, as it happened. Or maybe it didn't just happen.
Maybe that was part of the attraction: trying to do it right
under her nose, seeing just how close to her nose he could get.

So now the chase was happening right in front of her, scam-
pering buffoonishly through her own bedroom as if she, herself, were not there at all. The maid wasn't interested, thank
God. She was loyal to Rosina, and told her everything. The
count wanted to sleep with her. He wanted it more than he'd
ever wanted anything, that's what he'd said.

He must believe it too, Rosina thought. From the maid's
account, it sounded as though he was becoming almost a bully
about it, which was against his character, or at least against
the character he generally presented to the world. That character, the man he wished and professed and most of the time
managed to be—admirable, considerate, courtly—must be like
a too-tight shirt that had finally ripped at the seams. Now he'd

• • • • • •

pulled it off and left it lying on the floor, for someone else to pick up.

He was growing careless. He was grabbing at the maid in passageways, trying to pull her into corners. Starting out in a whisper, then raising his voice when she resisted. He bargained, threatened, pleaded. His eyes filled with tears. He bellowed. Everyone knew. He must have realized that Rosina knew too.

For several weeks she didn't leave her room. The household was swarming with hazards. Trysts, confrontations, conspiracies, exchanges of gossip. If she had gone out she would have seen things, heard things. She found it easier, though certainly not easy, to stay in her room, staring at the trees in the garden and at her own tired face in the mirror. She was sick of her own dignity, sick of pretending to be calm while the maid told her the latest incident, and sick with missing her husband—in the middle of all this, she missed him. It felt as though something were awry in him, some physical piece that had shaken loose, and if she could just get in there and tighten it up, he would be himself again, recognizable, and he would recognize her again too; he would shake his head and look at her and put his arms around her.

But she couldn't get anywhere near him. He addressed her formally, about estate and household business, on the rare occasions when they were alone together. He slept in a different part of the house. On nights when there were no dinner guests, she had a meal brought to her room on a tray, and he ate downstairs, watching soccer on TV.

Besides, what would she have said? "Please"?

He would have looked back at her and said blankly, "What?"

They were at an impasse.

What broke it, bizarrely, was that he accused her of having a lover. What? What? She would have laughed, if she hadn't

147

been so tired and heartsick and also afraid of him. He was furious—she'd never seen him so enraged. (He was project-ing, the psychiatrist she began seeing several years later would say. He wanted someone else, so he assumed you did too.) The purported lover was a young man, a kid, really, who worked in the house. He did have a crush on Rosina. Once when he came to her room to change a lightbulb, he gave her a poem he'd written: a wistful charting of the symptoms of love. He was so sweet; he could barely look at her. He came back to regrout the tiles around the tub. The railing on her balcony needed attention. "Am I in your way?" Rosina asked. "No, no, stay," he said. All right, she liked it; it was flattering and comforting to be worshipped a little bit. But that was as far as it went. "He's a child," she told her husband, when the startling accusation burst out of him.

"He's eighteen. He's a handyman. You're a married woman carrying on with the handyman."

And you're a married man who wants to fuck the maid, she could have said.

Oh, this was sordid, humiliating. It went on for weeks. In the end he said, "Rosina, please, I've been a complete jerk." It was his use of her name that melted her; she couldn't remem-ber the last time he'd said her name. Everything got cleaned up; everyone was bundled off. The handyman joined the army. The maid married her fiancé, who also worked on the estate, and the two of them were given the capital sum they needed to start a beauty salon and day spa in Seville.

Rosina had her husband back—but she didn't, not really. They were very careful. They had gone from "I love you" to "You see? I love you."

They went on a trip together to India. They came back and tried again to have a baby. He had a thing with one of the gar-

• • • • • •

dener's daughters, and possibly something with the graphic designer who did the labels for the wine. He told Rosina she was overreacting. "None of this means anything."

"I can't stand it," she said. "I may have to leave."

"You shouldn't," he said. "But it's your choice."

He was so patient. She, with her grievance, was so wearying. This is crazy, she thought, or else I'm crazy. She really wasn't sure anymore. He was calm and reasonable, and she was shaking, crying, listless, unable to eat or sleep. That's when she started seeing the shrink in Seville. He put her on an antidepressant and told her she was sane.

3

Elvira wasn't even interested in Johnny. He seduced her. He came to Burgos to scout for a movie. She was painting, working as a waitress. "My God," he said, when he came into the café with a couple of other guys for lunch. "You're amazing. What a face. Would you like to be in the film I'm making?"

She'd rolled her eyes at him and asked him what he wanted to eat.

"Food?" he'd said. "Who could think of food at such a moment?"

She laughed. She got suddenly that he was performing, making fun of this kind of scene. "I know," she said, writing on her pad. "You'll have an order of ambrosia, with nectar of the gods to drink."

"You got it, sweetie," Johnny said.

After lunch, when his cronies were leaving, he stayed behind and asked if he could see her that evening. She said, No, thanks. He came back that evening anyway. She said, No, really, please.

He asked if she'd meet him the next morning, before the café opened—

"Don't you have to work?" she said.

—so that he could see her paintings, in daylight.

"How do you know I paint?"

"I bribed a guy in the kitchen to tell me all about you."

She laughed. He made her laugh. It was a sad time for her—her mother had died a couple of months before, of breast cancer, at fifty-two. Elvira had lived at home for the last four months of that, and then had wanted to get away, anywhere. A friend from art school who was working in Burgos said there was plenty of work and it was a great place to paint. Fine, Elvira said. She was feeling dazed, unhinged. Burgos was fine. She could tell already that this was a period of her life she'd look back at someday and not remember; the days didn't feel real, each one was erased as soon as it was over. She couldn't remember last week. Her work was going badly: diligent, correct charcoal studies of stonework. She told herself to have faith, this at least was work, maybe these studies would coalesce and inspire something else, or would turn out to mean something in themselves. But she knew they stank. She would keep them, she kept all her work, but she would never want to look at them again.

This man, this skinny dark weather-beaten intense manic guy in the café, was like a giant mosquito suddenly buzzing around her face. She kept trying to swat him, but he kept buzzing, and for some reason this made her laugh. So she went out with him—which felt like something else she was doing now but wouldn't remember later. He asked again about her paintings, and she said they were lousy.

"I know what that's like," he said.

They were lying in bed at his hotel, smoking. With his free

· · · · · ·

hand he was stroking her head, over and over; it was very soothing. "Don't you like your movie?" she asked.

"I like my movie very much. It's going to be a wonderful movie. And we've definitely decided to shoot here. So: You want to come to Barcelona for a few months, while we do the preproduction stuff, or you just want to wait for me here?"

She laughed again.

"I'm serious," he said.

"No you're not."

"I am."

"Well, *I'm* not."

"Elvira," he said, "I'm falling in love with you."

"Stop it." She got up out of bed and started pulling on her clothes. "I just don't have the patience for this right now. I don't think it's funny."

"See? You say you're not serious, but you are."

"You're a very annoying person."

"Yeah, but you get me. Nobody else gets me. And I get you."

"Stop it, Johnny."

He rolled toward her, stretching out his arms. "You know I'm right." His face was soulful, pleading.

She relented, and laughed.

She went with him to Barcelona. What, was she going to remain steadfast to her waitressing job? Defend her commitment to sketching the bumps and crevices of the dusty stones that made up the walls of the castle of Burgos? She was still reeling from her mother's death, but a little better now. Awake, at least. She found a little apartment above a music store (mistake: the walls and floor, even the furniture, throbbed with bass notes all day and half the night), and a job in a gallery, where all she had to do was wear short skirts and black tights and answer a phone that never rang. Johnny stayed with her some nights, not others. He was silly, extravagant. Everything he did was a little, or extremely, embellished. One night she went to bed with him and woke up alone: on the kitchen table she found a card with a big letter *E* painted on it in gold. Very sweet; she smiled and forgot about it. But on her way to work another day, she happened to glance at the wall next to the token booth in the subway, and she saw a big golden *E* gleaming in the middle of the other graffiti there. She started noticing this gilded *E* all over the city, all along her route to work: on the sidewalk outside the café where she stopped for a quick coffee every morning, on the poster-filled brick wall next door to the gallery, and a very small one painted low on the stairway that led up to the front door.

He played the mandolin, and made up songs to sing to her. He liked to hold her in his lap and tell her an entirely preposterous version of what he had done that day—assassinations, space travel, stem-cell experiments, icing cakes for a royal wedding. He loved food and stayed skinny. He burped, farted, talked fast, said what he thought, asked for what he wanted, and was the happiest person she'd ever been to bed with. He was right there, not showing off, not acting, just happy. He was someone she might not have fallen in love with if she'd been older than twenty-four—but she was twenty-four, and she was crazy about him.

His movie was finished and got a lot of attention at festivals. Then it was released and it got even more attention. Johnny didn't seem surprised at any of this, but Elvira was; she had privately thought the successful-director thing was a kind of fantasy, more real than the wedding cakes and assassinations but basically along those same manically buoyant lines. Now he was rich, he was traveling. He didn't ask her to come

●　●　●　●　●　●

with him and Elvira didn't ask to go. Her work had become interesting—not the gallery job, which still paid her bills, but the painting. She'd graduated from stones to big pieces of buildings: the corner of a roof, a piece of bas-relief above a doorway, intersecting with the sky or a piece of pavement, and sliced off at unexpected angles by the edge of the canvas. She'd gotten her work into a group show, sold a couple of things.

Then one night she got into the bathtub with a stack of magazines—something Johnny had taught her; he said that reading in the bath was one of life's supreme pleasures—and in the front section of ¡Hola! she saw a picture of him with an actress. Wow, she thought, you made the tabloids. That's penetration.

Bad word, as it turned out. The caption said that Johnny was "linked" to the actress.

And that he was divorcing his wife of six years in order to marry her.

There was a smaller, black-and-white inset photo of Johnny with a different woman, whom the caption identified as the wife—his second wife.

Elvira got out of the bath and went over to the phone, naked. She stood there, dripping, with the phone in her hand and realized she had no idea where Johnny was, and no way to reach him. It was ten o'clock at night. She dialed his office and left her name and number on the switchboard answering machine. It's an emergency, she said. Please track him down and ask him to call me. She had been seeing Johnny for nearly three years, and this was the first demand she'd ever made. She had been incurious, independent—had noticed him noticing other women, but had never worried or even wondered about whether he did more than look. Work was the big thing in her life, work and then Johnny; she'd assumed that his life was a lot like hers.

He didn't call. What could he have said? And what could she have said—you asshole, you shithead, you prick? She left more messages at his office, always at night; if she couldn't talk to Johnny she wanted to talk to a machine, didn't want to have to deal with a real person who would only mirror back to her how crazy she sounded. You asshole. You shithead. You prick. You bastard. You liar. She went to the gallery; she came home. She smoked. She drank so much that one night she was standing at the kitchen table and the next thing she knew she was lying on her back on the bathroom floor, with blood on her forehead. She considered smashing the mandolin, which he'd left on the floor of her bedroom. She took a piece of paper and wrote on it, "Don't marry him. He lies," and wondered how to get it to the actress in Hollywood. She felt sorry for the wife. She studied their faces in ¡Hola! The actress was pale with red hair, fresh and certainly lovely, but with narrow blue eyes and a determined little mouth. A killer, Johnny. You've picked yourself a killer. Good. The wife was softer, older and, Elvira thought, more beautiful. Dark hair, dark eyes. An open face, an open-collar shirt. A man's shirt? Johnny's? With the tip of her forefinger she traced the planes of the wife's face. She got out a pad and some charcoal and made a sketch. She did another in pen and ink. She went in to her studio—she hadn't been there in weeks, since the night of the bath and the magazine—and spent a couple of nights painting the wife's face in oil, on a piece of board. Then she did the actress. That long white neck, that slash of lipstick.

A man came into the gallery one day just before it closed. *Johnny,* she thought (wistfully? Vengefully? She wasn't sure); but then she saw that it was in fact one of Johnny's friends— someone who worked in the office, a guy Johnny had known

*   *   *   *   *   *

forever, a Johnny wannabe, wearing a Johnny-esque leather jacket and skinny jeans. "You've got to stop calling," he said.

"Oh, really? Why is that?" Elvira asked. "Did Johnny send you?"

"Let's go get a beer. I want to talk to you. Really. I think I can put this whole thing into some perspective for you."

Tired, curious, lonely, and very much wanting the beer, she went with him. They sat at a sidewalk table under an umbrella. Elvira drank, smoked, shivered, listened to him, and at the end of it said, "And this is supposed to make me feel better?"

"My point is, this is just how Johnny is. Always has been. Always will be. He just loves women."

"Someone who really loved women wouldn't need to fuck so many of them."

"Okay, you're right. Part of it is the chase, the game. But look, he stayed with you two years—"

"Three."

"All right, even better. Three years. He must have cared about you to stay that long, right?"

"But according to you, he was screwing around behind my back that whole time. What did you tell me? *How* many did he sleep with when you guys were filming in Germany last summer?"

He held up his hand. "Stop shooting the messenger. I'm only the messenger."

"Well, thanks for the message," Elvira said, and she got up and left before he could make a pass at her.

"He gave me numbers," Elvira told Rosina, years later. This was several months into their friendship. They were driving together in Elvira's car, out to the country, where she had invited Rosina to come for lunch. "Actual numbers. They kept a list, he and Johnny. This many women in Turkey, this many in Germany. It was *statistical*. But crazy too. The numbers were delusional. A hundred in France, six hundred and forty in Italy. 'Stop,' I said. 'This is too much for me.' And you know what he said?"

"What?"

"He said, 'And you haven't even *heard* the news from Spain yet.'"

Rosina laughed; and Elvira did too, driving in that car with a good friend on a summer afternoon almost thirty years after these things had happened.

4

Here is a story: something I have not put into my memoirs. At least, not in this form, not yet. I have written six volumes so far, telling different stories, or changing and improving on the stories I have already told. My goal is entertainment, not veracity.

I had been living in Dresden, engaged in translating the Psalms and sleeping with my landlady and her two daughters. Each had her own attraction. The mother was avid, grateful, adept, and guilty; we played many operatic scenes of renunciation and reconciliation. The daughters were plump and rosy, and of course one was dark and one was fair, one tall and one tiny, one brazen and one aloof and trembling. But it was the triad that I found most alluring, far more than any of the three individually. The meat, the wine, and the sweet: together they make a satisfying dinner.

One night, very late, I came home to find my servant wait-

• • • • • •

ing for me in the street. He warned me not to go inside. The landlady, in one of her fits of penitence, had appealed to her brother for protection; and this brother, a gambler known for his violent temper, was waiting for me in my bedroom, armed, and in a rage all the more fiery because he himself had designs on one of his nieces. I heeded the warning and left that night for Vienna, taking with me only what I had in the pocket of my cloak: a little money and a letter from a Venetian poet and librettist praising my verses.

The letter did its work. The court composer to whom it was addressed welcomed me and recognized my poetic talent immediately, so that my first meeting with the emperor, which I had hoped would be an opportunity to petition him for a position, became instead an occasion to thank him for the one he had just bestowed on me. My life has been a series of inventions and reinventions, losses and reinstatements. This was perhaps one of the most successful, though it would not be the last.

At that time, Vienna was packed with composers, all clamoring for words. The Germans, the Italians, the French, and the English came asking me for stories, songs, dramatis personae. This week's sensation would be forgotten next week; always there was the desire for more, for something new. My first efforts contained little that was good. When my work was praised and I replied, "It is nothing," I was speaking not out of modesty but as one who is telling the truth. As for the music, it, too, was mediocre. I listened in vain for beauty, originality, taste, but heard only caution and ambition. And blame—when a new opera failed I was denounced not only by my rivals but by my collaborators. My fellow theater artists—that nest of stinging ants—contended that the music, the scenery, the singing, the costumes, all had excelled. It was my words that were at fault.

I learned and improved. My royal patron's faith in me was not misplaced. One of my operas met with tremendous approval, and I found myself in great demand at court and among the ladies. I was flooded with new commissions and amorous proposals, many of which I was forced to turn down but only in order to take full advantage of those I accepted. It was at this time that I lost my teeth, at the hands of a scoundrel posing as a dentist, enamored of a young lady who named me as her lover even though I had never met her. It was also at this time that I met, at a party, the small ethereal composer whose music owes its fame to several ears then in my possession: my own ear, which recognized immediately the quality of his music, and that of the emperor, which I had gained as a result of my recent great success.

The composer and I went to work. I sat up late, writing in my lodgings. The landlady's daughter—how dull my life, and my story, would have been without landladies and their daughters—was a silent, luscious girl of sixteen who would come to me whenever I rang my bell, bringing coffee, cake, and herself. Ding-ding! I would ring and she would come. I was forever hungry and thirsty. She kept me from my work, but she brought me what I needed to keep working. In the morning, not rested but unfailingly refreshed, I would dress and call on the composer. He and his wife (who, I cannot resist mentioning as an aside, was the daughter of one of his former landladies) would listen with delight to the words I had written, delight matched only by my own when he played for me the music to which he had set my words from the day before.

Those were the happiest days of my life, working at something while knowing how exceptional it was, not yet having finished it but knowing how beautiful it would be when finished.

•   •   •   •   •   •

Friends—musical artists—would drop by of an afternoon to listen to a small air on the piano, or to try out one of our new canzonettas. Bravo! they would cry. They were excited, they urged us to finish; but they were at a remove from us: eager spectators hanging over the fence. The composer and I were playing alone together with our characters and their yearnings and follies, in that delightful enclosure where the noble meets the ridiculous.

The reader will understand, and forgive me, if I embroider. The subsequent success of the work has perhaps colored my memory of its creation. Surely we quarreled? Surely we ventured down alleys that led nowhere? Surely the piece did not play itself out for us with perfect grace and ease as if we were its audience and not its makers? But it did. I vow to you, even allowing for a memory somewhat dimmed by age and sweetened by time, that it did.

And here you will permit me, reader, to digress upon the subject of memory. I have referred to previous volumes of my memoirs, through which perhaps the reader has already been gracious enough to roam, enjoying my earlier and somewhat varied accounts of my travels and accomplishments. I myself have not gone back to peruse them. They were written at a different period of my life—rather, at many different periods, inspired less by my need to remember than by my need for funds, and perhaps, if I am entirely truthful, by my wish for fame, and yet at the same time by a humble desire to share with others the many things I have seen and the many vacillations of my fortunes. Writing, and even more so, revising, has become my way of understanding and fixing my life, as a painter paints many layers and then fixes his colors with a glaze. Life is transitory. Words have the power to correct, conceal, and endure.

Who that has read Casanova's stories of his adventures can distinguish where his true glory lies: as an adventurer, or as a storyteller?

Yet although I have never reread these earlier volumes, I recall them well: with pride but also, I will confess here, with confusion and some unease. I recall that I have written elsewhere, in one of those earlier volumes, the phrase "Those were the happiest days of my life." I wrote that about the days I spent working on a different opera, with a different composer. At the time I lived those days, it was true. At the time, years later, when I wrote it, it was true. But now, fifty years after my time writing operas in Vienna, and thirty years after the publication of my first volume of memoir, I find myself considering and reconsidering these events and declamations yet again. Time and judgment collaborate to produce farce, and farce in turn contains much truth; major characters upon the stage may turn out to be lackeys in disguise, while the figures we have overlooked in the midst of much frenetic action unmask and reveal themselves as divinities. The piece I wrote with Martini that gave me such joy and triumphant gratification at the time of its creation and performance has been largely forgotten, while the ones on which Mozart and I worked are held in increasingly reverent esteem. I will not say that I have revised my memory accordingly, because I am not so easily swayed by the fickle judgments of others. But I have learned that memory is inconstant, which is perhaps its greatest danger and yet also its greatest virtue, the way in which it most truly mirrors our experience upon this earth. I have written within this very hour, of my collaboration with Mozart, "the happiest days of my life." If my wife were to walk into the room right now and ask me which of my days have been the happiest, I would tell her truthfully: "All the days I have spent with you."

• • • • • •

Having mentioned my good friend Casanova, I will end this digression by relating to you an amusing story that concerns him, and myself, and our respective (and, if I am honest about the way I regard it, competing) voluminous memoir series. The astute and indulgent reader may perhaps remember that in the third volume of my memoirs (which, I again assert, deserve to be, though have inexplicably not been, as widely read and celebrated as his) I spoke of a visit to my old friend, who was then living near Prague. My wife and I were on our wedding trip; she was fascinated to meet Casanova, and he, having of course an eye for female beauty and charm, both of which my wife exhibited in abundance, was extremely taken with her.

Writing of this visit in my memoirs, I refer to this gracious lady as "my wife," which she was. But I have heard that Casanova, recounting the same incident, speaks of a visit I made to him near Prague with my mistress.

What accounts for this discrepancy? Faulty memory? The shifting quality of experience, which allows the same scene to appear differently when viewed by different eyes? In this case, reader, there is no need to ponder these solemn questions about the inherent and treacherous pitfalls of memoir. The answer is much simpler. While I had intended to present my wife to Casanova with pride in my new married state, the sight of my old friend and fellow libertine made my courage falter. I remembered the many nights when he and I had gone out hunting together, the many conquests, the many mornings when we would stagger back to an inn or slip out through a back door, loudly assuring each other that we were two of a kind. I opened my mouth to request the honor of presenting my wife, and instead uttered words as far removed from matrimony as the devil is from heaven. Casanova was charmed; and my wife, who possesses not only beauty but also wisdom and humor, did nothing to disabuse him of the impression I had, in that moment of cowardice, conveyed to him. I invite you to laugh with me.

5

One night Rosina and Elvira went together to a dinner party given by a couple who had just bought two of Elvira's architectural paintings.

With the main course, the conversation turned to inheritance. A tall woman—an anesthesiologist who herself seemed sleepy—said that her cousin had just died without leaving a will, and that it was a mess. "His children are squabbling with the second wife, everyone wants everything, they're fighting over the paperbacks, over table linens. It's unbelievably ugly."

The man sitting next to her said that he dealt all the time with people who were trying to figure out how to allocate their estates. He was an archivist; he worked for one of the university libraries. "Famous people—writers, politicians, but also people who just have ordinary lives. We're interested in all of it—all the papers, all the artifacts. Even the things that don't interest us now may prove interesting in the future. If people aren't sure what to give us, I say, 'Give us everything. Just put it all in boxes and we'll take it.'"

"I have things in a box that I'm not sure what to do with," Elvira said. Rosina was startled: they had known each other for many years by then; it was the first time Elvira had ever mentioned this box. And the first time she'd spoken since they'd sat down to dinner.

"What kind of things?" the archivist asked.

. . . . . .

"When my mother died my father got rid of all her things," Elvira said. "Very quickly. Everything. Her clothes, her books. He threw out all her papers. She was an artist, she did watercolors. He got rid of everything in her studio, and he gave all her paintings away. I think he was so afraid of the pain of seeing any of her stuff that he just tried to erase her completely." Elvira picked up her glass and drank more wine. "But I would have liked to have kept some of it. I wish I had some of her paintings, or even little things. The china animals she had on her dresser, her gloves—they smelled like her perfume. He didn't even give us kids a chance to say if we wanted anything."

"That's terrible," the hostess said.

Elvira shook her head, her face creased. She could get into these intense moods, Rosina knew, where she tried too hard to make herself understood. "I'm not saying this to be critical of him—not after all this time. But it started me thinking about: What happens to all those little things? The ugly china animals—"

"The shells you picked up on the beach," the hostess cried.

"Who cares?" her husband said. "Who remembers? You're dead. Someone comes in afterward, sees a bunch of shells, and throws them out."

"But what if you picked them up when you were walking with someone you loved?" his wife said.

"Who cares?" he said again. The other guests looked away from them; something was happening between them that was too much for the dinner party.

Elvira ignored it. "So I started to put some things into a box. I've had it for years. I wouldn't show it to anyone, there's nothing in it that would mean anything to anyone else. But my question is, what do I do with it?"

"Bury it," the anesthesiologist said. "Take it out in the woods somewhere. Or leave instructions to have it buried with you, when you die."

"Give it to us," said the archivist.

"Leave it to someone who you know will treasure it," said the hostess, speaking softly but managing somehow to convey an air of miffed defiance of her husband. "Do you have any nieces and nephews?"

"If you give it to us, you know it will be preserved," the archivist said.

"But I don't want to try to make sure it will be treasured, or preserved," Elvira said. "I want it to go to someone, but where I won't have any idea what will happen to it. It needs to be a risk. I want to make a decision that somehow ensures the box just has to take its chances."

6

Here is the rest of what Rosina knew, by now, about Elvira and Johnny.

They had not seen each other again for sixteen years, after she found out about the first wife and the second wife and the future wife and all the other women. Then they ran into each other at an artists' colony. "Well," he said when they first saw each other the day he arrived with a script he wanted to revise, "I've been wondering when this would happen." He reached for her hands and she automatically gave them to him.

What had he said next? She couldn't remember. She remembered that the conversation had been very brief, that he'd been warm and confidential, that she'd been laconic almost to the point of sarcasm, and that she'd had a confused sense that he

· · · · · ·

was evading her—her knowledge of him—by being direct. You see? his manner said. I am exactly what I appear to be. I'm not hiding anything. No tricks. "I follow your work," he told her. "I send away for the catalog when I know you're having a show. And whenever I'm in L.A., I go and visit your picture at LACMA—the one with the—well, I don't need to tell you which one it is."

Oh, come on, she thought, while at the same time unwillingly thawed by the flattery. Just as she was warning herself to be careful, he squeezed her hands, deepened his smile, and then let go of her and walked away. *Don't you dare try any of your shit with me,* she said silently to his receding back. She was amused to realize that if he didn't try any of his shit with her, she was going to be annoyed. Annoyed is okay, she told herself, just don't let it get anywhere near despair.

All that first week, she watched him operate. At dinner he would sit between two women and somehow manage to gaze into the eyes of both of them. He had lost most of his hair; he had thickened and creased and roughened some, so that what had been tender and melting now looked tough and weary. But the eyes; the smile; the hands; the voice; the warmth; the keen, energetic, happy sympathy with whatever was said to him; the quick, jumpy humor—all his deadliest weapons—were the same.

It was interesting (more than interesting, intoxicating almost) to watch all this with detachment, to realize that after all this time she really was just a spectator. But he was making mincemeat of the women in the colony. One told her boyfriend from home, who had been planning to visit, not to come; she needed time to think. Another spoke of leaving her husband and small son. Whenever Elvira walked through the colony's main living room, there were women draped on couches, crying; women hunched in the phone booths; women asking if anyone had any pills for a migraine. Elvira spent a lot of her time, when she should have been working, giving these women tea in her studio and trying to warn them, to explain Johnny to them. "I knew him a long time ago, we were together . . . ," she would say. The women listened to her eagerly, with tears in their eyes, wanting help; but the story didn't help them, it didn't stop them. The more she told it, the cheaper it felt.

"Johnny," she said to him one night, "you have to stop this."

They were standing outside together on the terrace, smoking. It was the one time Elvira allowed herself to smoke all day, and the one time she allowed herself to be with Johnny—these little moments after dinner, in the darkness, when he came up to her and asked to bum a cigarette.

"Really," she said, when he didn't answer. "You're hurting people."

How had that led them back into each other's arms? Elvira couldn't remember, she told Rosina.

But it was very gentle, rueful. It was older-but-wiser sex. It was two old opponents laying down their arms. It was the unicorn putting his head down in my lap. It was me being immune to all the old bullshit, and falling for a whole new set of bullshit. It was believing I knew him through and through, and that that would keep me safe. It was thinking that out of all those women, I was the one who had endured for him, and that maybe it had been my job to endure all the others. It was loving him, even though there wasn't much about him that I could respect or admire.

In the end I did get hurt again. Not as badly, it wasn't as violent as the first time. I had been curious to see: Can I do this? Will having my eyes open make it possible to do this? And in the end the answer was no, not really.

I'm not sorry, though, that we tried again. We tried for about a year. I know what he's like. But I've never been happier than I was when I was with him.

Here's something else, something I have never talked about and don't like to think about. While I was there, at that colony, I did paintings of some of the women, the ones Johnny was fooling around with. I was fooling around, too, just experimenting with these little portraits. (Although I did sleep with two of the women—another experiment. And another story.) It made me remember, though I hadn't thought about it in years, the pictures I'd done of Johnny's wife and that actress. Those two I had painted in a rage, in despair, wanting to confront those women, to own them, to swallow them, to take them over— I don't know what it was; it was crazy. The portraits I did at the colony came out of something quieter, more deliberate. Curiosity. Still obsessive, I suppose—in some way I was trying to see through Johnny's eyes, to be Johnny, to find what animated each of the women. The tough little performance artist with the dyed-black hair. The nervous young playwright. The eighty-six-year-old sculptor—Johnny kissed her in the laundry room while she was moving her clothes from the washer to the dryer; she had a serene, lively face, and such lovely, smooth skin.

Anyway, when I got home, I kept doing little oil sketches of women's faces. Sometimes if I'd been with Johnny and noticed him looking at a waitress or someone we walked past on the street, I'd paint that person. Or friends of his, actresses he'd worked with, anyone I thought he might have made a pass at. But mostly I just painted anonymous women, from life or from photographs in magazines. The point after a while wasn't *Who had Johnny slept with?* It was *Who might Johnny sleep with? Who would he want to sleep with?* In other words, all women. Each woman. What would Johnny see, if he looked at this one, or this one?

It sounds crazy, I know. But I was happy, doing those paintings.

It didn't keep being about Johnny. After a while the work wasn't about him anymore; I barely thought of him when I did it, except as a kind of joke: Hey, Johnny, your horrible friend gave me your big catalog of women; well, here's mine. But I was in love with the pictures themselves, the fun and interest of doing them, all those women.

The next time I had a show, I planned it as usual around the architectural paintings. Those have always provided a living for me—good in some years, in others pretty scant. But there is a long alcove off the main space in the gallery where I show my work, and I decided to fill it with some of these small pictures of women. The show got only one review, a short one, which praised the large paintings but referred to the portraits as "trite, solipsistic wallpaper" and suggested I stick to painting buildings.

I should have a thicker skin by now, but I guess I don't. Those were thin-skinned pictures.

7

And what Elvira knew by now about Rosina: A few years after she and her husband had divorced, she had fallen in love. The handyman, who had adored her all those years ago, had returned from the army. He looked her up, and came to visit her in the apartment where she was then living in Seville. She began the affair out of a kind of tired, residual, martyrish spite toward her ex-husband, even though they weren't in touch anymore. You thought this is what I was doing? Fine, then, I'll do it.

But the young man was kind, loving, steadfast.

They had never married, but they'd been happy together for ten years. Then he'd been killed in a skiing accident, and she had moved away, with their son.

8

Friendly reader! Though why I begin this chapter with these words I do not know, as I am fairly certain that what I write here will be crumpled up and thrown into the fire before any reader, friendly or otherwise, has been permitted to see it.

Given the voluminous size of my memoirs, and the frequency with which further installments have been issued by the publisher, the reader may perhaps doubt my ability to view any of the words I write as less than indispensable. But I assure you: as much as there is, there could have been more. I add, remembering and inventing; and I subtract, when in the rereading something strikes me as unworthy: too small, a private memory that would only be diminished, were I to publish it. The story I am about to recount here may be excised later not because it is too sensational but because I may judge that it is not sensational enough.

It concerns a night spent in Mozart's company. I have written elsewhere of the second opera he and I wrote together, and of the disappointing reception it received in Vienna, after its initial triumph in Prague. In Prague they cheered; in Vienna they yawned and caviled. I have written that Mozart responded to the emperor's remarks on the occasion with great poise—that when the emperor said that the Viennese did not seem to have the teeth for this music, Mozart suggested equally that they be given a little more time to chew on it. In truth Mozart said nothing of the kind. I wasn't there to overhear whatever he said to the emperor. I was in the alley behind the opera house, parting company with my dinner. I'm sure that Mozart's actual conversation with the emperor was perfectly polite and innocuous, if perhaps less pithy than the exchange I invented for publication. I am equally sure that it had nothing to do with Mozart's real feelings on that night.

What Mozart said to me, when I told him that the emperor had opined that the Viennese hadn't the teeth for the music, was, "Then they can eat shit." We were sitting up late that same night in my lodgings, and we had sent the servant out for punch, once, twice, and a third time. We went over the performance, the glory of the music, the grandeur and buffoonery of the drama. We recalled the delightful time we'd had writing the opera in Prague, with my old friend Casanova looking over our shoulders and providing unnecessary but vivid advice on seduction techniques and the strategies a rake might employ to escape from a tight corner. We dwelt bitterly on the inexplicably chilly reception our beautiful creation had that night received. Vienna's indifference felt like cruelty, mockery.

The conversation began to wander. I told him of the occasion when I was young and first began to write verses, and a boy who was my friend came up behind me as I sat at my desk, snatched away the paper on which I was writing, and read aloud my ode in deep, overwrought, satirical tones. I was angry at my friend—whom I ceased to call by the word—but even more I was humiliated. He had caught me in a moment of tenderness and passion, doing something I was proud of and wanted publicized but which was also deeply secret to me,

. . . . . .

deeply serious in a way that did not require anyone's approval but could ill withstand anyone's mockery.

Mozart, in turn, told me that when he was little more than a boy he had fallen in love with a beautiful young singer who returned his feelings. He left for a period of several years, to travel and give concerts. When he returned, not much richer but as much in love as ever, he went to a gathering at which he knew the young lady would be present. He wore his best red coat, thinking as he donned it how grand it would make him look in her eyes. But while he had been gone, she had become a celebrated singer and had been taken up by a protector who had both enriched and hardened her. At the soiree she ignored him; when he approached she was too haughty to talk to him, but turned instead to her cavalier and made fun of Mozart's red coat.

He laughed a little, after he told me this story; and I laughed too, to remember my despair when my treacherous boyhood friend was dancing around the room, declaiming my verses and waving the paper out of my reach. We drank more punch. We noted with philosophical wisdom that these hurts go deep, but he had loved again and I was still writing. What we did not say was that with these hurts an edge is worn down. It happens out of necessity—it would not be safe to carry a knife that sharp. But something is lost too: that early, perfect, impractical sharpness, which is so beautiful but which cannot survive being seen.

We felt better after that night. The work was performed again, and its greatness was gradually admitted.

One more brief addition, before I end. A story went around that someone had asked Mozart how he intended to refute his detractors.

"I will refute them with new works," he said.

It was a confident, valiant thing for him to say, everyone thought. I thought so too, when I invented the story; and I still believe it today.

9

When Elvira dies, in her early sixties of a heart attack, she will leave her house and her money to her brothers, and all the contents of her studio to Rosina.

It will be almost a year before Rosina can make herself go out there, and then only because one of the brothers calls to say the family is trying to get the place ready to sell. She knows by now that grief is mostly endurance, understanding over and over that the person you loved is not coming back. The drive itself smites her: the dull, flat landscape around the highway, the orchards, the two falling-down farmhouses with trees growing in the middle of them, the village—passing these things that used to mean she was getting closer to Elvira, all the landmarks, not remembered for so long but now seen again and remembered perfectly.

She cries in the car, and dreads driving up to the house itself; but by the time she arrives she is calmer. No one is there. It's a strange, sultry afternoon in August: the sky a molten pewter, and the light is white, fierce, burning. The silence, too, is immense. She walks through the high grass—nothing tragic here, it was that way when Elvira was alive; she never cared about cutting it—to the barn and opens the padlock with the key that came in the mail from Elvira's lawyer.

She knows the inside of Elvira's house by heart. The

• • • • • •

smoke-blackened wall above the living room fireplace, the kitchen with its sagging cupboard doors, the toppling piles of frayed towels in the linen closet, and the fresh smell of the sheets on the small bed in the guest room and on Elvira's wide bed, where they sometimes spent nights talking in the darkness until they both fell asleep. Rosina was never sure what that meant to Elvira, whose feelings for her might have had a romantic piece. If it was true, she was pretty sure there hadn't been any suffering involved, though she also knew that believing this was easier than admitting the possibility of anything different.

Yet with all the time she spent in the house, she's been in the studio only once, early in the friendship. When she flips on the lights that August afternoon, she will see a vast, whitewashed, raftered space, crammed with stuff, neither neat nor messy, just occupied-looking. This will choke her again, sting her eyes. It looks just like what it is: a workroom someone walked out of one afternoon, expecting to be back the next morning. Magazines lying open, pens uncapped, a mug with a tea bag trailing out of it, an address book, a crumpled tissue. There is a painting on the easel, and next to it a table jumbled with paints. Crusted brushes in a crusted glass. The canvas is a small one, about seven inches square: a woman's face. A direct gaze, hair pulled back but with pieces coming loose around the face, a funny asymmetrical half smile, lips slightly parted. Impossible to tell her age: Elvira hadn't painted her skin yet. Rosina will be surprised to find this picture. She had thought, from the way Elvira had told her the story of that disastrous show, that she'd stopped doing these paintings of women.

But what she finds next surprises her even more. Dozens of these small portraits, hundreds of them, stacked in the plywood shelving that fills the old horse stalls. The big paintings of buildings are here, but most of what's here are these women, painted steadily and in utter privacy, apparently for years.

So now there will be years of trying to get these pictures shown. Arranging to have them photographed. Cataloging them. Creating a binder. Writing a description of the show. Naming it: in the end Rosina decides on "1172 Women," which, astonishingly, is how many there are, and she feels strongly that they all need to be seen together, at least to begin with. What was wrong with Elvira's earlier show, she decides—aside from the fact that the critic was an asshole—was that there weren't enough pictures shown. The paintings are individually lovely; but it's the quantity that is crazily beautiful, the dogged, obsessive, insatiable, repetitive power of face after face after face.

Nobody wants it. Nobody has room for it. Finally there's a happy, or happy enough, ending. A woman Rosina sits next to at an opera fund-raising lunch mentions that she has a friend who directs a museum at a college in Texas. Rosina mentions the pictures, the woman offers an introduction to her friend, and eventually the paintings travel (Rosina charters the plane), are shown, are reviewed and praised. Then they travel back, and Rosina puts them into storage. She will keep trying to find them a permanent home.

But before any of that happens, Elvira's house will be sold and the studio emptied. There are a few boxes piled against one wall: books, old sketchbooks, Christmas ornaments. And one box—just a regular brown cardboard box like the others, but this one taped shut—with a piece of paper taped on top of it. A note:

Rosina—This is the box I was talking about that night at the Cristinos' dinner party. E.

•   •   •   •   •   •

Rosina will take this box home with her (the rest go into storage for now), and will consider for some weeks what to do with it. She will think of opening it. She will think of keeping it and never opening it. She will not remember Elvira's exact words, but she knows it was something about how the box needed to take its chances, that it needed to go to someone who would do something unforeseen with it. She will remember Elvira talking about happiness, about the times of her life when she was most happy.

Rosina will take a piece of paper and think about what to write on it. *Voi che sapete. Voi sapete.*

Then she'll decide the hell with it, and she will send the box, with no note, off to what seemed to be the latest in the long string of addresses Elvira had written down for Johnny.

• • • • • • •

The News from Spain

Some of this is fiction, and some isn't.

At the age of almost sixty, I fell in love with a man who wasn't my husband. And I loved my husband very much. We were in a long, happy marriage, had raised three children, still wanted each other (we would leave work and meet at home some-times, at lunch). Enough context—more would begin to sound self-righteous. I fell in love with someone else.

Nothing happened. I was married; he was married. We worked together. I could say that we were lawyers, or doctors who shared a suite of offices, or that we had adjacent chairs in the string section of an orchestra, or that he was a painter and I ran the gallery, or that I was the painter. But any of that would be an invention, and that's not the kind of fiction I'm interested in. What I will say is that we worked together closely for many years, and the work was something that mattered to both of us. It wasn't as if I got a crush on my squash partner, and could then prudently decide to play squash less often or find a different person to play with. Each of us had strong reasons to stay there, to keep seeing each other, even after our feelings—mine, anyway; I was never quite sure how he felt—made themselves known.

Such coy, evasive, passive, pseudo-Victorian syntax! "Made themselves known"—as if these feelings had their own lives apart from us, their own dilemmas about how to behave. Should they continue to shuffle around quietly, wearing slippers, in order not to disturb us; or should they stand in the doorway and clear their throats until we had to look up and acknowledge their presence?

My feelings were quiet for a long time. I didn't even know they were there. There was no instant attraction. For several years I liked this man, admired him, respected him, trusted him. He paid attention to whatever he was doing, and he was kind, but rigorous too. I liked where his tolerances and intolerances fell. I thought his jokes were funny.

Then I realized I had started to look at the floor whenever there was a silence between us; I had trouble looking directly at him. I imagined us cooking together: an excellent omelet. I imagined him kissing me; imagined us in bed. When I went to a concert or a museum, I imagined running into him, or going there with him, listening to his smart comments—imagining this while in reality I was there with my husband, listening to *his* smart comments.

Was I alone in feeling as I did? This, always, was the question. If the man, my colleague, had given me any of the usual small signals of seduction—sizzle glances, accidental brushings against—I would have recoiled, and the attraction would have ended right then. But he was correct. Warm, though. Very warm. The way he looked at me, some things he said. I was going away alone on a trip, and he said, not once but twice, "I wish I could go with you." And there were other things, occasional remarks that lit me up and made me wonder.

My feelings—let's hold on to this idea of them as shuffling Victorians, let's make them servants, an entire uniformed household staff—were fresh, raw, perpetually startled. They weren't sensible. But they behaved themselves for a while. They were frank, earthy even, among themselves; but they were discreet. They kept their mouths shut and their faces neutral. They never did anything to embarrass me or give me away. They had been trained; as long as they stayed in their own part of the house and I paid their wages—a ridiculously small sum, but they didn't know any better, so I could get away with it—we did well enough together. They were invisible, I wasn't even required to know their names. I underestimated their docility and overestimated my own power, and, like all fables about arrogance, this one turned menacing.

My feelings started to become unruly. Maybe they read something that stirred them up (a revolutionary pamphlet, handed to them on a street corner as they strolled past on their afternoon out), or maybe they just grumbled a lot and egged one another on, nursing the teapot in the servants' dining room. They came to me and said, in a tone that was not insolent but not entirely respectful either, that they wanted more.

You will be noticing, about now, that these servants are something of a threat not only to my peace of mind but to this story. Dangerous as prospective household mutineers, they are more dangerous as a metaphor. Here, too, they want to take over. Now that they've intruded, it's tempting to stay with them, this charming, scoundrelly bunch of domestic malcontents, to name them and give them rooms in the attic and possessions and mothers and sweethearts. I could keep writing about them, and allow myself to be distracted—rescued—from the hard thing I meant to write about. So I am ordering them back to the kitchen. They shuffle down the corridor and through the baize door, obedient for now, but there may be trouble later. There's trouble already. I want them shut away but I heard what they said: they wanted more.

I needed to tell the man how I felt about him. I needed it for a long time—months—without doing anything about it. But then I couldn't stand not to anymore. I know: bad idea. Naming something makes it real, unignorable, gives it power. (So, too, does refusing to name something. I don't want to give this man a fictional name—Pete, Edward, and see? He is instantly diminished—so I'll just call him A. It shrinks him a little, but he's mostly intact, and it's better than the self-importantly secretive and clumsy "this man.") I needed to tell A how I felt. We were sitting together in his office one afternoon, working, with the door shut. I told him that I loved him.

He looked at me.

What had I wanted? Not for him to get up and cross the room and take me in his arms. But to see things in his face. Joy. Love that matched mine. Relief that I'd said it out loud for both of us.

But what I saw in his face was nothing. Blankness—as when you mistakenly think you recognize someone on the street and you smile and wave and the person looks back at you: *Huh?*

The silence went on. We stared at each other. Finally I said I was sorry.

"No, no, no, no," he said. His face had unfrozen. There was an expression on it: his forehead was creased; he looked troubled, dismayed. "Please don't."

Don't what—love you? Say it aloud? Apologize? It was too

late; I had already done all three. And the excruciating politeness of that "please"! We continued to sit there.

"I'm sorry," I said again; and he said again—although this
time at least he omitted the courtesy—"Don't."

Somehow I got out of there. I had work to do, he had work
to do. My daughter was expecting her first baby and I was
taking her shopping, to some store out by the malls. She was
much bigger than she'd been when I'd seen her last. Her hem
was uneven: high in the front and drooping in the back. She
was wearing low, old shoes. I wanted to hug her, for that hem
and those shoes. We looked at the crib she'd seen before and
thought she liked, and then we walked up and down several
other rows of cribs. "I hate them all," she said. She looked at
me and she was starting to cry. "Why do they make this stuff
so ugly?"

I put my arm around her.

"Will I still be the same?" she asked. "Do things ever go
back to how they were?"

"No," I said.

I bought her all the stuff—the crib, the changing table, the
stroller. We had tea. I heard everything she said. Things felt
clearer and more vivid than they usually did, as if I'd been
purged somehow by my humiliating afternoon with A. I wasn't
thinking about it or remembering it, but it was there, hurting
in the distance. Once, in high school, I sprained my ankle during a dance in the first act of *Guys and Dolls*. It hurt, but the pain
also waited for me: it agreed to let me get through the rest of
the show before it said, "Now."

This pain, the pain about A, hit me, unsurprisingly, later
that night, when I was in bed next to my husband. I had been
lying there with a book, my eyes moving over the lines of type,
not reading. I was aware suddenly of my husband's stillness,

. . . .

and aware also that he'd been still for a while. I looked over and saw that he'd fallen asleep. His book was on his chest; it had shut itself around his hand. He was still wearing his glasses. I got out of bed and went around to his side, took the book and the glasses, turned out the light. I touched him lightly on the shoulder, and without waking he slid down in the bed so that he was lying flat.

I stood looking down at his sleeping face. He would not have told another woman "I love you." If he knew I had said it to A, he would have been terribly hurt. He wouldn't have understood it. But he would have forgiven me. He would have trusted me not to—not to what? Not to sleep with A? There was no question of sleeping with A—I knew that, and my husband would have known that. My husband would have trusted me not to go any further than I had, not to do anything worse than confess my feelings to A. He would have trusted me not to sit there with A exchanging longing looks, and having brave trembling conversations about love and desire and frustration and honor, and sighing together, "If only . . ." Having romantic feelings was one thing; conducting a romance, even an unconsummated one, was another. The line was there. I saw it and would not have crossed it. Good. Right. Got it.

Yet I had crossed a line when I told A I loved him. And I wanted those things that lay across the line—those trashy shameful taboo things: sighs, confessions, endearments, eloquently articulated longings. Or rather I wanted agreement from A that these things could have happened. I did not need to play them out, or even to soulfully renounce them—I just needed him to say, "Yes. You're right. There's something here, and I see it too." I had thought I'd needed it, anyway. Now I thought I'd be happy if we could just forget I'd ever opened my mouth.

I went downstairs and got out the bottle of cognac and poured myself a glass. (All the thick wadding of years of heedless domesticity: my husband's cognac; the cut-glass tumbler part of a set my children and I found one long-ago summer at a Rhode Island flea market where we also bought my son a box of lead Napoleonic soldiers; my slippers a gift from my mother-in-law.) I sat in the dark living room with my legs tucked under me.

I can't describe how I felt then, except to say that I needed to make myself very drunk. My feelings were rioting, they'd become an angry mob, they'd pulled out all the knives and come pounding through the house looking for me.

I do remember thinking, with that clarity you can sometimes feel when getting drunk, that when A said "Please don't"—oh, God, the memory of his creased white face!—what he meant was don't talk about it. Don't make it explicit, you'll kill it. Whether or not he had loved me before—and it seemed to me, now, that he had, quietly and steadily, in exactly the way I would have wanted him to—he certainly wouldn't from now on. By speaking, I had turned myself into a problem.

And I remember wondering—and drinking more, this was when I tipped over into oblivion—what A was doing right then: sleeping with his arms wrapped around his sleeping wife; awake and working, not thinking of me; awake and sitting in his own dark living room, drinking cognac and thinking, Shit. How do I handle her?

Humiliation. Humiliation was the big one, the butler, the majordomo. He was a bully, with cold eyes. The others were afraid of him. He ran the house.

.   .   .

Years ago, a friend told me she'd had an affair. She fell in love with a man who kept breaking up with her because he felt guilty about his wife. My friend would have understood that, she said—she felt guilty about her husband—but the unbearable thing was that the man could make himself break it off only by deciding my friend was a terrible person. He railed against her, blamed her, disavowed every loving thing he'd ever said to her. She was devastated. Then, months later, he would start it up again—the flirting, the heat, the desperate pursuit, the secret conversations and meetings.

After this happened a few times, she told him she wanted to end it for good, but that she wanted it to happen kindly. She wanted them to sit down together, remember the good things, and say good-bye. She thought that with this mature acknowledgment, she could let him go. Without it, she felt stuck, helpless; she was perpetually being pulled toward him or pushed away. Please, please could he just give her the calm and loving good-bye.

But he never did. He came to visit her in the hospital after she had brain surgery. He'd brought her flowers. She could hardly see, but she was touched to know that he was there. "You are such a fucking bitch, you know that?" he ended up saying, sitting next to her bed in the neurosurgery intensive care unit.

The next day I bustled around and got many things done. Look how effective I was, how resilient. I didn't see A until the afternoon, when we had our usual meeting to go over things in his office. I was a little jumpier than usual; he was more quiet.

"Look," he said finally. "We should talk about it." His voice was low and deliberate; his blue gaze was steady. I had not been imagining things, he told me. But there was love, and then there was what you did about it. "For instance," he said, "running off with you to a foreign city would be the most unloving thing I could do."

"Oh, but it would be fun, though," I said quickly. Then I said, "I know."

Then we sat there and smiled at each other for a while—each still safely on our own side of the line, but the line wasn't there in that long moment, the wall was down—and then we went on talking, easily now, about our work.

Oh, it was beautifully done, I thought later. I had stopped on my way home to walk near the river for a while. Beautifully done by both of us, but especially by him. He was beautiful. He'd saved everything—love, honesty, my dignity. He hadn't been a prude or a seducer. He'd said what was necessary, and had said nothing that wasn't. The perfectly judged understatement of it!

And yet—understatement? "Running off with you to a foreign city"—that was a blurt, not carefully considered. As reckless, in its way, as my own passionate confession had been the day before. And it was his image, not mine. I had never said anything about running off, or conjured up a foreign city.

So he thought about me too. He imagined the two of us on a night plane, checking into a hotel, white sheets, a bored waiter, beautiful old streets, different smells and tastes, different light, a different river.

It was an early spring evening, the river rough and choppy, the rowers pulling hard on their oars. Runners came toward me and went past. Next to the path the road was clogged with headlights, cars barely moving.

Or maybe he was making a point of exaggerating, throwing

●　●　●　●　●　●　●

out something so absurd that I couldn't possibly make the mistake of taking it seriously. "A foreign city," he'd said—maybe he was being sarcastic. We can't exactly go to the moon together, someone might say, without harboring, or expecting to trigger, any fantasies of craters and dust and extreme cold and zero gravity.

I went home, where my husband was happy to see me. I don't actually remember any details of this particular evening with him, but he was always happy to see me. He would have asked about my day, and I would have told him about parts of it. He would have told me about his day. I must have cooked something and we ate it, maybe by candlelight. He cleaned up the kitchen.

I took a long bath that night. I lay in the hot scented water and thought, A loves me. A told me he loves me. I thought about the foreign city, chose it rather than the moon. But the moon kept pushing its way back in. I knew what A had meant, but I didn't, quite. It wouldn't hold still; a little more clarity would have fixed it securely in place. God, you women, the butler said, coming into the room where he should not have been, looking down at my naked body with contempt. I got out of the bath shivering and wrapped myself in a towel. A loves me, I tried to think; but each time I thought it, the elation and surprise of it were a little less, the uncertainty a little greater.

At work the next day, A smiled at me. He smiled all through the next week. Warm smiles: the same kind he'd always given me. But something was withheld too. "Thank you," he said, where in the past he would have said, "Thanks—you're terrific. But since when is that news?" I began writing scripts for him. What he would have said if I had not made my declaration. The lovely words I might have heard if I hadn't craved even lovelier ones.

But my scripts went further. They were wistful, but also peeved: the words that ought to be said by a man who has told a woman he'd like to run off with her to a foreign city. I knew why he wasn't saying them—our marriages, our working together, that clear bright line that we both saw and would not have crossed—but I wanted him to somehow give me the words without saying them, the way spies and fugitives in movies mouth words to each other silently because they know the room is bugged.

A story, or an essay, can become close, airless. You cannot stay shut up in your own head anymore; you need a break, some fresh air. Let's go outside. We'll take a walk, down a New York City side street. It's 1944. Women in high heels are out walking small shivering dogs. Uniformed maids push old men in wheelchairs. Garbage day: the cans are out. The slow trucks, with garbage men jumping off, hauling, emptying, trotting, whistling, and jumping on again, block the street, but there isn't a lot of traffic. When you drive to where you want to go, you can park. Not a lot of garbage either; the last fifteen years have been about saving, not discarding.

The doctor parks and hurries from his car. The patient's condition is not serious—although he would not say that for sure until after he has examined her—but she is one of several patients he is going to see this morning. He is always busy, he always hurries; but he has never had a patient who would not have said of him, "He is so careful—he sees everything."

He rings the bell and waits on the stoop, holding his black bag. Someone inside the house pulls open the door: the most famous woman in the world. What is she doing there? It's like a dream: I got on the ferry and the pilot was Joan of Arc, and then Winston Churchill came along and punched my ticket. But he pulls himself together instantly, takes off his hat and transfers it quickly to his left hand, the one holding the bag, so that he can take her proffered right hand with his own. "Come in," she says. "I'm glad you're here."

He follows her up the stairs. Already he has observed some things about her. Some extra weight in the torso. Slight osteoporosis. She is very tall, erect, yet droopy. But tremendous energy and intelligence: she is recognizably the person he has read about. She looks like her pictures—he almost wants to laugh at how familiar she looks, and sounds, that quavering patrician fluty voice he's heard so often on the radio. But she is different, too, like a painting that you have seen reproduced many times in books but have never stood before until now: the colors brighter and clearer than you had imagined, the depths more withdrawn, the canvas huge, a whole audacious wall's worth, when you had expected something tamer.

She leads him to his patient's bedroom. The patient, a woman he has treated for several years, thanks him for coming. Already he is holding her wrist, looking at her eyes and skin tone. She introduces the famous woman (the doctor nods, his fingers palpating beneath the jaw), an old friend, apparently, who has come to nurse her.

"Well, you needed someone," the famous woman says, walking over to the window. "And there are so few civilian nurses these days." She holds the cord of the blinds. "More light? More privacy?"

"Light, please." The doctor continues to examine the patient. The famous woman adjusts the slats and watches him. He is deft, thorough. His hands, which she would have expected to be steady—he looks like a man with steady hands—are trembling slightly. Nerves? Some kind of illness, a palsy? No, she decides, continuing to watch him. He shakes because he is concentrating so hard. He has a fine, serious face. She knows doctors, her husband's many doctors—some who have promised too much and been proven slowly wrong; some whose pessimism is like a fortress, without a door or even a window, so that she, though not usually prone to hysteria, has felt like a madwoman running up and down beside the thick stone walls looking for a way out or a way in, a way to get somewhere other than where she is, standing with the eminent somber doctor who keeps shaking his big, hopeless head. This one, the young man listening now with a stethoscope to her friend's difficult breathing, is quick and sensitive.

She watches him pack up his bag. "So now you have some work to do, but nothing to worry about," he says. He leaves medicine and instructions, and then follows her back down the stairs; his tread behind her is light, almost noiseless. "Would you stay for some tea?" she asks him.

For the first time she sees his smile. Oh. Not just a good doctor, a good man. "I would like to, very much. But I have several more patients to see this morning, and I'm afraid I'm already late."

"I understand," she says, moving briskly to the door—of course, he's very busy, she mustn't keep him. She holds out her hand; he takes it and bows over it. She watches him clap his hat on as he hurries down the steps to the sidewalk, before she closes the door and goes to the kitchen to make tea for her friend.

The doctor, walking back to his car, wonders if it was a mistake to refuse the tea. How gauche, to say no to her! It must not happen very often. Well, that fellow certainly is full of himself, she must have thought as she closed the door. But he knows, somehow, that she would not have thought badly of

. . . .

him, that she understood about the patients and the lateness. The pressing schedule does matter, but it also, now, seems foolish. Would another half hour have made that much difference? He gets into his car and drives away, regretting the lost chance to sit and talk with her.

A year later, after her husband's death, the famous woman telephones him. She has moved from Washington to New York and does not have a doctor here: Would he be willing to take her on as a patient? He would be happy and extremely honored, he says, improvising a gracious little speech, to which she replies, with what might be either self-effacement or tartness—or both—"Don't worry, I won't take up much of your time. I'm very healthy."

She proves herself right on both counts: he never sees her. Eventually she comes to him for shots before an overseas trip. He suggests a complete physical; it has been a while since she's had one. Not necessary, she says. He understands, then, what it is to oppose her, the stubborn force of her. She cannot be pushed. But, he thinks, she has an open mind: she listens, she can sometimes be convinced. He explains that a doctor needs a baseline, in order to stay alert to any deviation. "I know how strong you are, and it's in both our interests to help you stay that way. But for me to do my job I need information." He smiles at her. "Think of it as a fact-finding mission."

"Fine." She begins unbuttoning her dress.

He has wondered if perhaps she is especially modest, or even ashamed of her body, which might account for the reluctance to be examined. But it turns out that no, in fact she is entirely at ease and unself-conscious. The cloth gown falls from her shoulders and she ignores it, sitting bare-breasted on the examining table, chatting away, falling silent only when he leans in and listens, after asking her to breathe deeply. He is the one who is self-conscious, or rather conscious of her, of the body. Of all bodies, suddenly, no one is immune: their sagging and slumping, their softening, their improbable fortitude and inevitable weakness, their gallant, long, doomed struggle against failure. He is not a sentimentalist, but the sound of her heart, pumping resolutely and privately beneath the white mottled skin of her chest, nearly brings him to tears. *Healthy female, age sixty-two,* he begins noting on a chart in his imagination; he has collected himself, and gently tells her she can get dressed. She's in great shape.

This time the tartness is unmistakable. "What did I tell you?"

He collapses, a year after that. He has to go to Switzerland, to leave everything: New York, his practice, his little girl. And his wife. The chest X-ray is at once sentence and manumission.

He writes to inform his patients; and the famous woman, that great helper of people in trouble, calls to say she is flying to Geneva, and she has arranged for him to have space on her plane. He thanks her. There are things he wrestles with, but not the fact of illness, a patient's or his own. A bacillus is a fact. Help is offered; you take it.

The plane judders and buzzes. The sky is black. The silver clouds are enticing: a carpet. You could get out and walk on it. He is cold and hot, wrapped in a blanket. The lights are out, people are sleeping. She sits next to him and they talk. "It's late, you should sleep," they murmur to each other sometimes, after a silence, but they don't sleep. By the time they come down in Newfoundland in the gray morning, they have told each other everything.

The stop is too long—the scheduled refueling, but then an engine problem. In the afternoon they get back on the plane, and now he does sleep. She sits and watches him, his thin face

. . . .

damp with sweat, bruise-colored shadows under his eyes.
When he wakes, he looks confused.

"Almost there," she whispers.

"Almost where?"

"Shannon."

It's the second refueling stop. But something goes wrong
here too; they are not called to reboard the plane. Fog, she is
told. It's midnight. Ordinarily, at such a delay, she would take
some papers out of her case, or start talking with the workers
in the aerodrome. But the doctor is slumped in his chair, shivering. She touches his forehead with the back of her hand and
then with her palm. Then she does what she almost never does:
makes a fuss. Someone comes with a lantern and leads them
down a dark road—a mile, they walk it, freezing—to a cold,
empty barracks, rows of bare bunk beds.

They are there together for four days. It's like a shipwreck.

Afterward they go on to Switzerland—she to the long days
of meetings, careful, patient, an old diplomat among other old
diplomats, wisely keeping the horse, who wants to gallop, to
a walk; and he to the clinic with its terrace full of deck chairs
overlooking the mountains. He lies there and writes to her,
wearing sunglasses and fingerless gloves; he has plenty of time
for letters. She doesn't have time but she writes to him anyway,
late at night in her hotel room.

She loves him. She says it trustingly, the way she bared herself on his examination table. She doesn't hide, or apologize,
or seduce, or provoke. She doesn't try to dazzle or amaze; she
has no particular interest in the sound of her voice. She doesn't
demand anything; in fact she is anxious to assure him that
there will be no demands. She is an old woman in love with
a younger man, and she is a realist. She'd like to see him and
hear from him sometimes. She doesn't cringe, but she doesn't

want to take up too much space. She just wants him to allow himself to matter to her, to matter more than anyone else does, or has, or will.

What do you do with such a gift? The doctor slits open her envelopes in the alpine sunlight of his clinic bedroom. Her words might unnerve him, but they don't. He doesn't have to check or caution her, because she has been so swift to check and caution herself. There is nothing to explain. Oh, the grace of her, the humility and courage. He is free to speak of love without saying more than he can honestly say.

When she is dead, her daughter will find his letters and burn them in the bedroom fireplace.

Now we have to go inside again, away from the bright bracing Swiss winter air and back into the overheated office where A and I did our work. The room where we sat together—his office—must have been beautiful once, and still had some straggling remnants of architectural dignity. Over the years it had become deeply familiar to me. The high ceiling, with an empty plaster acanthus wreath at its center and a breast-shaped protuberance covering the hole where a chandelier must once have been. The blocked-up fireplace. Two tall windows, A's books and papers on the wide sills, the parquet warped and stained pale beneath the old silver radiator. His coat on a hanger on the back of the door: a raincoat in the fall; in winter a parka or a dark gray overcoat, depending on where he might be going that day during lunch or after work; then in spring the raincoat again; and now, in early summer, nothing. Just the pale wooden hanger, stenciled with the name of a store too faint for me to read.

I had been away for two weeks, helping my daughter and

her husband with the baby. He was tiny, exhausted a lot of the time; but already you could see that he was a person of good sense and great curiosity. My husband and I sat with him on the living room couch while our daughter showered or tried to sleep. We talked to the baby as he lay stretched out along our thighs. "He's listening," my husband and I said to each other. "Look. He's trying to figure everything out." We smiled at him and at each other, shaking our heads.

"How was it?" A asked. He already had a grandchild; he was ready to marvel with me.

"Fine." I didn't want to talk about it. I had constructed something, or restored it, over the past two weeks; I'd been living with my husband and family in a solid house on a green island, and I wanted to keep A, with his understanding smile, away from it. I wanted to keep myself straight. A was the man I worked with—familiar, dear, beloved even, but he was in his place. Good. Stay there.

But he smiled, and I smiled. Soon—within a week or two—we had found our way back to each other. He was telling me about his granddaughter's birthday party, and I showed him pictures of my grandson. He said, "His eyes are like yours."

Who knew that this could happen? This mating dance that would never lead to mating, this circling in slow deep rhythm around photographs of grandchildren. I laughed and forgave us. We were in love; we didn't have to talk about it; no one needed to get hurt; we were at a resting place.

And it might have been fine, if I could only have rested there. I wanted so badly to be the woman to whom you could give an inch knowing she would never try to take a mile. But even more than that, I wanted the mile. A, I said, you know what I told you once, and do you remember you told me you felt the same way?

He was angry. I feel like you want some sort of pledge from me, he said.

At home the butler waited, holding his razor strop, swinging it against his leg.

I am writing about women, about love and humiliation. Men do it to us, but mostly we do it to ourselves. We love the wrong people; we love at the wrong time. We think that we can make it right, reconcile the irreconcilable. We are like game-show contestants who don't know when to stop. We could go home right now with the money and the washing machine, but we want the car so we keep going and we get the answer wrong, or choose the wrong door, or spin the wheel too hard, and then we have to go home with nothing.

Back now to the doctor. His TB is gone, he's healthy again. It's 1950. He is vacationing in Cuernavaca with his wife and daughter. What excuse does he give them, how does he manage to slip away to call on a journalist late one night? The journalist, who is waiting for the doctor in her house, doesn't care how he manages it, as long as he comes to her.

They met at a party earlier that evening. They knew of each other's existence, through the famous woman who is his patient and her friend (and idol, except that the journalist isn't much of an idolizer. Say rather that the famous woman is someone she admires very much and whose good opinion she values). "I've heard so much about you," they said, and laughed at the dopiness of that. They talked all evening; the other guests paled. "Come walk with me," she said. His face was close to hers; he took the lit cigarette from between her fingers and stepped

· · · · · · ·

on it before she'd had a chance to smoke it. Now there's a soft scratching at her door. She hasn't turned the lights on, she's been waiting for him in the dark. It's a bright, hot, starry night. He kisses her, he murmurs to her, he fills her, she can't get him close enough. He—but wait. You know how this goes.

She knows how it goes, too, only for her it has never gone that way. The men pound away with their peculiar urgency, their eyes shut tight, their whole selves shut tight, and she's shut tight too—isn't this supposed to be open? Is she doing it wrong, or does everyone lie when they describe it? And all the stuff leading up to it—the smooth wooing that always sounds like a line (she sees right through it, it's the men themselves who seem to believe it; when she has, occasionally, interrupted to tell them, in extremely plain language, what she understands them to be driving at, they look shocked and hurt, except for the good ones who have laughed and taken her straight off to bed), the passionate declarations, the cajoling, the bullying, the appeals to her sense of responsibility (men and their needs), the appeals to her sense of guilt (she made them want her and now she owes them, they bought her drinks and dinners in a war zone where there wasn't a whole lot to drink or eat and now she owes them). She is perfectly capable of saying no, and has, plenty of times, charmingly, or politely, or accompanied by a slap or a slug, whatever it takes; but a lot of the time she's said yes. She's been curious, or lonely, or she loved them, or she felt sorry for them—sorry because she liked them as men and hated to see them putting themselves through all the hoops. *Stop*, she always wanted to say, as her hands moved to unbutton her blouse, *not necessary. It's no big deal.* And it wasn't. She thought it probably wasn't that big a deal to the men either, at least not overall. They wanted it until they got it; then they forgot about it until they wanted it again. But it was supposed to matter, and it didn't, which made her uneasy when she thought about it so she didn't think about it.

Now, in bed with this man, she wants to shout. It's what he's doing to her—things no one else has done, except for a few who, she always thought, were trying to prove how unselfish or worldly they were; they asked afterward if it had been good and she said yes and had to restrain herself from congratulating them, which was what they really seemed to want—but more it's that she suddenly, finally, for the first time, gets it. She takes his face in her hands and looks up at him, astonished. "I know," he says. And he does know: she believes he knows everything.

He leaves, he has to. First just for a few hours, to go and do whatever it is he has to do in that other part of his life, the vacation with the pretty daughter and the depressed, depressing wife; he slips back to see her, though, again and again in the next few days. Then he has to get on a plane to New York. Come back, come back, come back. She's sore, hoarse, shaken, hungry: Could anyone possibly keep this up? Come back, she says, and he's laughing, and crying too, kissing her mouth and her hair; but she's thinking also that maybe it's good that he's leaving. She needs a break, to write, to think out what this is.

What is it, what is it? She writes pages, a letter to him. She walks away from it but then picks it up again an hour or two later and writes more. She puts the pages in a drawer. She can't send it. It's too long, too much, it would capsize him. She's been a writer for twenty years, she knows her own voice—but this is a voice she is hearing for the first time. She has never been able to quite believe in anything until she has seen it for herself and found the language to describe it. Poverty and starvation in America, war in Spain. And now, out of nowhere, love. It shocks her and dazzles her, this new voice; she gazes at it and topples over into the pool of it and drowns.

．　．　．　．　．　．　．

When he comes back for a weekend, two weeks later, it's the same. The days, the nights. No family this time: he is hers, uninterrupted. They eat, they swim, they keep going to bed. She's a terrible cook. They laugh about this. He feeds her an orange, section by section.

What would it be like to live this way? he keeps saying.

Like this, she says. It would be just like this.

My God, imagine.

We don't have to imagine. We're here. You'll come live with me, you'll—

Work?

Why not?

My patients, my practice—

There are sick people here, too, you know.

Well, then, that's settled, he says, reaching for her again. I'll just move here. That was easy.

See?

He leaves, he comes back. More sun, more oranges, more talk—and it's serious now—of how they will live. He'll have a clinic a few days a week. The rest of the time he'll just be with her. He'll write—he has always wanted to write. You'd write terrific books, she tells him. She knows: she writes terrific books, and she used to be married to one of the great writers. The doctor is intimidated by the idea of her former husband. Those are big shoes to try to fill, he has said.

Yeah, she said—well, his shoes and his ego were the biggest things about him.

It's kind of nice, having to reassure the doctor about something. The men who boast and swagger always need to be taken care of; but the doctor, who doesn't show off his muscles, is strong. It's nice that there are a couple of chinks, some endearing vulnerabilities. *I would never hurt you,* she tells him silently, *even if I have to lie to you.* But in fact, she is never tempted to hurt him, and she doesn't need to lie. She'll be his for as long as he wants her. She hopes it's forever, but if it isn't, she'll live.

She writes to her friend, the famous woman. And here is a different voice: halting, but clean and pure. (She imagines herself and the doctor as children—no, young lovers. Juliet and Romeo without poison, without a dagger, going hand in hand to their parents to ask for a blessing. This is nuts and she knows it. She and the doctor are both in their forties.) She waits apprehensively for an answer. She can almost write it herself: *You need to remember that he is married, with a child.*

The famous woman writes back swiftly. But not about the doctor's marriage; the rebuke is about his work. Why would you think of asking him to move to Mexico? He is established here in New York, and very dedicated; his work is important. It's the woman's job to mold to the man. You are in Mexico only on a whim. Why should you not be the one to move? You could write anywhere. It would be selfish to ask him to give up what matters to him for the sake of a childish reverie.

The journalist throws this letter away, to free herself of its frosty cadences.

The famous woman, in New York, paces her bedroom late at night, wearing a mud-colored chenille bathrobe. He has rendered unto her the things that are hers—but there are things that will never be hers, no matter how badly she might want them. He has never promised more. It is her job to control her own appetite. She doesn't daydream about Mexican beaches or mountains. But she has imagined the two of them, each alone (maybe he stays in his marriage, maybe not: he's alone either way), working hard separately—but connected, always, by a strong current that runs between them, a mutual frequency heard always, and only, by them. He's a young, healthy man in an unhappy marriage; she accepts (tries to accept) that he will seek companionship, maybe love of a sort, with young women. But not this: this engulfing fevered wasteful stupid enslavement, this utter forsaking of himself to pursue some dream that, she suspects, isn't even really his dream. If he goes she will lose him. She tells herself—she really believes it—that what's more terrible is that he will lose himself. But she knows that trying to hold on to him would only be a different way of losing him.

She remembers the four days in Ireland better than he does—he was so sick there, so helpless. She remembers walking to get food for him, a mile in the fog, the road invisible in front of her and behind her, just the sounds of her footsteps and her breathing. There might have been fields full of sheep, or disused airplanes, or houses: she never knew. There must have been people—the other passengers from the plane, the people she bought the food from—but all she can remember is the fog hiding everything, and the way he looked lying on the bed. She made a private place for him in a corner, hanging blankets to cordon it off. He ate like an obedient child.

Her room, this bedroom, is big and homely. Things are here not for beauty but for a reason: the lamps to read by, the books for information and ideas, the photographs on the wall for love. A wall of pictures: her children and grandchildren, her friends, her dead husband and father. The doctor's photo is by itself, on the table next to her bed. Her great feat in this love is to be unashamed.

He flies down to Mexico again and again. The journalist welcomes him, loves him, starts to know him better. He's a worrier. He wants to talk it through, over and over. He's been offered the directorship of a polio hospital just outside New York. It would be such a good post for him, would combine so many of his interests. But she has said she can't write in New York. He will turn it down, but he needs to think. He will move to Mexico, definitely, but it will take time; things need to be worked out. Enough reassurance from her and maybe he will really do it.

But she doesn't want to attain him by assuaging his doubts. She wants this to be free of doubt, clean. She wants it to be the way it was at first, when he came shooting toward her like an arrow. Stop dithering, she tells him sharply; and then has to clean up the mess of having hurt him. But the mess keeps spreading; the more she scrubs, the bigger it gets.

Now he is taking steps—he opens a Mexican bank account—to prove to her that he is serious. If he were really serious, he wouldn't have to do all this proving; he would move and let things figure themselves out. She has done it that way, many times in her life: you know where you want to be, Paris, Washington, Madrid, Germany, and you go there, period. He wants her, but not enough.

It's all right, she can let him go. But she can really love him, now, only if he does go.

This is her failure, not his. There's a hardness about her. She has always known, but hoped it might change. It did change for a while when she met him, but now it's back again and without the hope: if he couldn't change it, nothing ever will. This is a sad piece of knowledge, she finds once she gets through the initial pain of losing him, but not dire. She did love him, and still does. And what she really loves, anyway, is work.

Two women who both love the same man: it's hard not to take sides. The journalist never knew there was a contest. If she had, I think she might have felt compassion for the famous woman, tenderness, even though the journalist was so tough, and even though she never spent much time thinking about whether her acquisition of a man might be leaving some other woman bereft. I don't think she would have acted any differently—she wanted the doctor very badly—but she would have admired the famous woman's fortitude and pragmatism, and the sheer gutsiness of loving so deeply and improbably. Or maybe not. Maybe the journalist did know how the famous woman felt, and was sorry, but not that sorry. You pays your money and you takes your chances. Or maybe she knew and thought it pathetic and ridiculous, an old lady's ravenous longing for a handsome young man. Excuse me, your desire is showing—the way you might tell someone that her slip is showing, to save her from humiliation.

It's all speculation. These people are dead—if they were ever real people to begin with. I'm hedging, describing them without giving them names. You can figure out who I mean, but you'd be making a mistake if you were to confuse these characters with those personages. People leave clues but keep many more things secret. I'm trying to find my way inside, insinuating myself through the hairline cracks, starting with something real and ending up with fiction. A love story—your own or anyone else's—is interior, hidden. It can never be accurately reported, only imagined. It is all dreams and invention. It's guesswork.

Having said that, before I circle back to my own bewildering history with A, I'll tell you one more thing, and this really did happen. Two years after she and the doctor parted, the journalist spent some time in Italy. She heard that the famous woman was staying nearby. Things had been cooler between them since the affair with the doctor; the journalist missed the old warmth and approbation. She hoped to patch things up, and drove over one day to say hello. What she didn't know was that he would be there; he was traveling with the famous woman as her doctor. The sight of him shook the journalist. He was still the same, and he still looked at her the same way. Well, of course not the same, but it was enough for the two of them to go off to spend the night together. The famous woman didn't like it; they would have seen that, if they'd been looking in her direction. Maybe it's as well that they didn't look.

So what was my story with A? "Uneventful," I want to say. "Nothing happened." Certainly there was no geographic sweep to it—no Ireland, no Mexico, no journeys along the Adriatic coast. Not even a brief business trip. I imagined it sometimes, how a trip like that might go. I'd reined myself in, after those first incontinent declarations. I didn't dream of a foreign city or a romantic hotel, or even, any longer, of us in bed together. Just an overnight stay away, in a place of irreproachable tameness. Cleveland, say. The Hilton. Separate rooms. Sitting up together late at night, in one of the hotel's public spaces—a dark bar off the lobby. We would talk. Nothing else would happen—but it would have been a talk that acknowledged and illuminated and calmed everything. Away from our lives, on a high bluff over-looking the entire low-lying plain of the landscape, we would have been completely frank and open with each other.

But the nature of our work was that we never got away. We didn't ever go anywhere. We sat in A's office, going over what had been done and what still had to be done in the coming week or month or year. We reviewed, we planned. The great sweep of our story wasn't geography, it was time. We sat there for years.

Then one Saturday afternoon I was in a lingerie store downtown. I tried on different things, looking at myself in the fitting room mirror, trying to imagine which combination my husband would like best. When I carried the pieces—embroidered, scant, expensive—over to the sales desk, I saw the identical garments already lying on the counter. I turned to smile at the man who was buying them. It was A.

I had met his wife a few times over the years—she was a little older than he, a big, forthright, scrubbed-looking retired family lawyer who now did volunteer work for assorted nonprofits. The things A was buying would not have fit her.

"Thanks, nothing quite worked," I managed to say to the saleswoman, and I fled—the store; the sexy little pieces, which were tainted now and were too young for me anyway, really; and most of all A's face.

It was a three-day weekend. No office until Tuesday. It was like being shredded from the inside. I had lost my parents, and my mother-in-law, whom I loved; had lost friends to cancer and a car accident; had watched friends suffering their own losses. And had watched the news, read the papers, knew what pain there was in the world. Romantic pain, when you're in your seventh decade and happily married, should not be this brutal, this consuming. That weekend we took our grandson, who was now three, to a goat farm in the country. The goats stepped up a ramp onto a little carousel, three goats at a time, to be milked. Our grandson asked questions, petted the goats, hated the cheese. He wanted to know why goat's milk tasted different from cow's milk, and what other kinds of milk there were. I smiled at him and let my husband try to answer the questions: I didn't know.

A was waiting for me on Tuesday morning, his face grave and wary. We went into his office and he closed the door. We sat in our usual chairs facing each other. His marriage was rough, he said. His wife had been a drunk for years. She'd been violent with him; she had repeatedly threatened suicide. He did not feel able to leave her. "I'm not going to catalog it all for you," he said, "or try to justify myself. I just want you to understand a little, what it's been like." Twelve years ago—before I knew him—he'd met someone. "It's a complicated set of loyalties," he said.

"It must be," I said. The two women, the two hidden lives. "A, I'm sorry."

"Don't be." He smiled at me. "I'm not unhappy." His shirt was one my husband owned too—a pattern of thin and thick blue stripes. Both my husband and A had worn this shirt for years. I knew what the cloth felt like; I had taken it to the cleaner's many times. I saw the mistake I had made, thinking that in some small but real way A belonged to me. My love for him was foolish, a kind of vanity, as well as a disservice to him: it had nothing to do with who he was. He had had agonies, and made accommodations, and found love and comfort—that was the real, deep river of his life, flowing along through land I'd never seen.

I stood up to go. "I'm glad you told me," I said, which wasn't quite true but felt nearly true in that moment: a beneficent compassion for him, for me, for his wife and for the younger—I knew she must be younger—woman.

"Thank you," A said.

I wanted to lay my palm lightly for a moment against the side of his face, but A and I had never touched each other since we'd shaken hands the first time we'd met.

That night my husband and I went to a concert; an old friend, a violinist, was playing in Telemann's *Paris Quartets*. The music was formal, orderly. I was flying apart. For the purpose of narrative unity, it occurs to me to return to the servant

• • • • • • •

metaphor—to invoke again those evil retainers, to add new members to the staff, who were by now holding me captive, doing whatever they wanted. Rage: a stable boy, unwashed, wild, brutal, very strong, barely capable of speech. Shame: the housekeeper, a tight-lipped woman dressed in black with sparse greasy scraped-back hair, who hissed excited filth at me and watched—to guard against impropriety, she said—while the butler stripped me naked and beat me. But while it might be structurally correct to resurrect the metaphor, it's tonally off. Too neat, too distant. Making something safe, when its unsafeness was the most essential thing about it.

The next day I called in sick, and the day after that too. I was trying to protect myself, but also to protect A from the force of what I was feeling. On Friday I pulled myself together and went in, but he was out that day, having a colonoscopy. Good, I thought. I hoped he would be all right, that they wouldn't find anything; but I also hoped that the prep had been miserable.

I saw A on Monday and we moved on, back into our usual work. But then he asked after my grandson, and I said coldly, "He's fine."

A said, "Tell me what he's like now."

And I snapped, "Whom would I be telling?"

Oh, lady. Hide yourself. You are dangerous, crazy, outsized, and out of control. It isn't this man's fault that you fell in love with him. You imagined that he loved you too, when he was just being gallant. It's not his job to help you get over it. You always knew that his first allegiance was to another person—what difference does it make to discover that the other person wasn't who you thought it was? It still is not, and never would have been, you. And anyway, your first allegiance isn't, and never has been, to him.

You want, you want, you want. You don't even know what it is you want.

He was hurt. I could see it, and also saw that he regretted hurting me. But he wasn't angry, and he didn't point out that I had no right to feel injured, no reason to trust him less. We tip-toed around for a while, a couple of months. There was a sadness between us, I thought, a wary fragile solicitude. Finally—he was being very kind, and even though I was mostly behaving well, I did snap at him now and then—I said one afternoon in his office, "Just give me a little room." He nodded. He knew what I meant. But I needed in that moment to be unguarded with him, to be utterly clear. "Getting over unrequited love is harder than I thought it would be."

A said, "What makes you think it's unrequited?"

Another friend told me, years after it happened, that at one point she had met someone and fallen deeply, quickly, passionately in love. The man did too, but he broke it off almost immediately because he felt guilty about his wife. My friend understood; she felt guilty about her husband. She did write to the man several more times, even though he had told her not to. She couldn't help herself. Each time he wrote back, kindly but tersely: *We can't.* Then one morning, a year or so later, she was reading the paper. The obituary section. She went for a long walk, a lot of long walks. There was no one to tell.

You meet someone, you fall in love, you marry. You meet someone, you fall in love, it turns into a disaster. You meet someone, you fall in love, but one of you is married, or both are: you have or don't have an affair. You meet someone, you fall in

• • • • • • •

love, but you are never quite sure if your feelings are returned. You meet someone, you fall in love but you are able to keep your feelings mostly hidden; occasionally they cough, or break a dinner plate, or burn down the kitchen (accidentally? On purpose?), but mostly they stay out of sight when other people are around. At night they have the run of the house. It's a creepy, even sinister, ménage. An outsider who happened to glimpse it might be horrified—might ask you in a whisper if you needed to be rescued: Wouldn't you like to call in the authorities? But no, you're fine. It's your own lunatic household; you know how everything works. You've all been together for so long that the servants have acquired a battered credibility. They've endeared themselves without ever having become likable. You respect one another's endurance.

A and I still work together. There's nothing new to report. Things happen: half declarations, cautious withdrawals, sudden flare-ups, gradual repairs. It reminds me of that old late-night comedy bit, repeated every Saturday night: The news from Spain this week is that Generalissimo Francisco Franco is still dead.

When things didn't work out between the doctor and the journalist, he accepted the job as director of the polio hospital on the Hudson. Sometime in the 1950s my grandmother went to work there as a physical therapist, and she fell in love with him.

I don't know much about it: my mother mentioned it once, years ago, and I wasn't paying attention. I do know that the doctor was married, to his second wife—a happy marriage, unlike his first one.

Watching him moving toward this second marriage must have been hard for the famous woman. It wasn't like the affair with the journalist, when she could wish for it to end because she could see how bad it was for him. This time the doctor was happy, and deeply loved. The famous woman embraced it for him—the courtship, the girl. Not perfectly: she grumbled and was cool sometimes (the new wife, to whom it would never have occurred that this renowned figure might have feelings other than those of devoted, even maternal, friendship, was baffled by the occasional chill), but overall the famous woman accepted with grace. When they got engaged she withdrew for a little while, but then reappeared and held the wedding in her living room. Every year after that she gave a cocktail party for the doctor and his wife, on their anniversary. After my mother died, I found an invitation to one of these evenings tucked inside a biography of the famous woman, which must have once belonged to my grandmother.

"She loved him for years," my mother said about my grandmother. I don't think anything ever happened. I remember my grandmother as strong, solitary, independent: a stoic with a wry sense of humor. It was hard to imagine her abject, pining.

Maybe she wasn't. Maybe the doctor returned her feelings. Maybe he didn't return her feelings and she was philosophical about it. I like to think of her going to work every day and concentrating with him on doing as much as could be done for those patients, noticing small increments of progress, knowing not to expect too much.

Acknowledgments

Warm thanks to the MacDowell Colony and Yaddo, where the book was written.

And to the National Endowment for the Arts and the Massachusetts Cultural Council.

And to Gordon Lish and George Andreou.

And to Jay.

A NOTE ABOUT THE AUTHOR

Joan Wickersham was born in New York City. She is the author of two previous books, most recently *The Suicide Index,* a National Book Award finalist. Her fiction has appeared in *The Best American Short Stories* and *The Best American Nonrequired Reading.* Her op-ed column appears regularly in *The Boston Globe;* she has published essays and reviews in the *Los Angeles Times* and the *International Herald Tribune;* and she has contributed on-air essays to National Public Radio. She has received fellowships from the National Endowment for the Arts, the Mac-Dowell Colony, and Yaddo. She lives in Cambridge, Massachusetts, with her husband and two sons.

A NOTE ON THE TYPE

This book was set in Monotype Dante, a typeface designed by Giovanni Mardersteig (1892–1977). Its first use was in an edition of Boccaccio's *Trattatello in laude di Dante* that appeared in 1954. Although modeled on the Aldine type used for Pietro Cardinal Bembo's treatise *De Aetna* in 1495, Dante is a thoroughly modern interpretation of the venerable face.

Typeset by Scribe, Philadelphia, Pennsylvania

Printed and bound by RR Donnelley, Harrisonburg, Virginia

Designed by Maggie Hinders